THEN CAME WANDA... WITH A BABY CARRIAGE

DAKOTA CASSIDY

COPYRIGHT

Then Came Wanda... with a Baby Carriage (Book 15 Accidentally Paranormal Series)

ISBN: 9781720223092
Imprint: Independently published

ACKNOWLEDGMENTS

Darling readers,

Please be advised, this is an Accidental Quickie, wherein our incredibly patient, all-things-good-and-kind, always-a-lady Wanda fights for a family of her own. The series is, after all, about three strong, empowered, badass women, each very different from the other. Yet fiercely in agreement upon what it means to be the force that drives your life's happiness, while still surrounding yourself with friendships and family. That will always be my focus, but on that note, I get a fair amount of email about the girls' life mates, Keegan, Greg, and Heath.

So I thought these quickies were a fun way to touch base with the Accidental men, who are often left at home to tend to family matters, while keeping the OOPS girls growing and moving forward as the years pass. It's a lot to put in one book with so many characters to keep track of as the Accidentals grow in size. So a short novella seemed the way to go.

Which brings me to this particular installment and its shorter length, done in the manner of *How Nina Got Her Fang Back*. This won't be one of our typical Accidental adventures, in the sense that a new hero and heroine are introduced with an accidental turning. Though, we do have a couple needing help, and as always, there'll be plenty of mayhem, whacky madness, and of course, love and everlasting friendship!

Thank you for joining the ever-growing Accidental family with me time and time again. You'll never know how deeply your dedication to this series touches my heart.

Most of all, this book is dedicated to my oldest son, Travis. As an adopted child myself, I always knew someday I'd want to adopt, too. You have no idea how blessed I felt from the very moment I laid eyes on you in 1990 in that hospital in Alexandria, Romania, when you were just six months old. To this day, almost twenty-seven years later, words still can't define the depth of my joy or my love from the second I held you, and every day since.

Yet, the ultimate thanks go out to your birth mother, who so selflessly offered you an opportunity she, due to circumstances beyond her control, was unable to provide. She was courageous, kind, loving, and humble. She is, and always will be, the woman who gave me one of the greatest gifts I could have ever wished for.

You.

Love,

Mom XXOO

THEN CAME WANDA... WITH A BABY CARRIAGE

BY DAKOTA CASSIDY

CHAPTER 1

"Who's the best, handsomest, loudest little dude in the whole wide, wide world?" Nina Blackman-Statleon cooed at the tiny bundle tucked close to Wanda Schwartz Jefferson's chest, nuzzling her nose against his cheek.

Baby Schwartz-Jefferson, as yet still officially unnamed, due to the nature of his rushed placement with his new parents, responded in kind by balling his fists, opening his mouth wide and howling louder, the tint of his pale green skin turning a muddy red with his frustration.

Nina clucked her tongue and scratched her head full of luscious dark hair before grabbing his small fist and pressing it to her cheek. "Dude? You're howlin' like your skin's peeling off. Auntie Nina just wants to make it better. Help me help you, little man."

"Maybe he's teething? Charlie's been perpetually teething for what seems like an eternity," Greg

Statleon, the gorgeous husband of the equally gorgeous Nina, suggested hopefully, waving a round teething ring fresh from the freezer in his hand.

"The truth," Nina muttered in agreement. She took the teething ring from Greg and brushed it against the baby's mouth, but he made a sputtering noise, scrunched his face back up again and returned to his caterwauling without missing a note.

"But he's too young to teeth," the woman named Marty said.

Nina made a face at her other friend. "What's too young in this crazy flippin' world we live in, Marty? Charlie's been teething for almost three years now because she's half vampire and ages slow AF. The witch half of her is setting her twenty billion stuffed unicorns on fire on the reg, and making it rain in the playroom with thunder and lightning like she's been doin' it for a hundred years. Little dude is paranormal, is all I'm saying. Might wake up tomorrow and find he has a full set of teeth."

Wanda tightened her hold on the squirming infant, looking helplessly to her friends from her seat on the rocking chair she'd received at her impromptu baby shower only three days ago.

"*What* am I doing wrong?" she whispered, her pretty eyes filling with plump tears. "I've rocked, walked, bounced him until my legs are ready to fall off. I've offered him the milk and powdered food they sent home with us from the orphanage, but he spits it right back out. Nothing works! He's been doing this for hours. Maybe it's just me? Maybe...maybe he hates me."

Marty Flaherty gripped her friend's slender shoulders and hugged her hard from behind, her bangle bracelets jingling and shiny around her slender wrist. "Who could hate you, honey? No one. That's who. So just forget that notion right now. He's just adjusting to his new surroundings, that's all. He's been in a different environment for almost a month of his life. This is all new. New smells, new sounds, new everything."

Nina bobbed her head emphatically, clinging to the baby's fist with one hand and using the other to brush a tear from her friend's face. "What Marty said. He might only be a month old, but I'm sure he senses the difference in routine, people, whatthefluff ever. Okay, so he senses it in an excruciatingly loud way with lungs the size of Sherman tanks, but the little dude's just expressing himself. He's as new to you as you are to him, Wanda. Swear, that's probably all it is, dude."

Marty paused and looked to her friend, cocking her swirly blonde head with the immaculate highlights. "Did you just agree with me, Dark Overlord of the Night?"

"She did," said the tiny black cat with an enormous head (Calamity, to anyone who asked) curled up in a ball on the back of an overstuffed armchair by the bay window.

Nina covered the baby's ears and narrowed her charcoal-black gaze at Marty. "Shut your gooped-up face, ass-sniffer, and you, too, Calamity. Yeah, I agreed with you, numbnuts. And if it meant this super unhappy little dude would stop crying, I'd even shop with you. Wear makeup. Put on a stinkin' dress. A fucking *yellow* one with flowers and lace. Whatever it takes."

Marty snickered and grinned. "Marshmallow."

Nina recovered the baby's ears with her fingers. "Frosted blue eyeshadow-aholic," she shot back.

Marty stuck her tongue out at the half vampire, half witch, visibly fighting not to respond out of obvious respect for the baby's tender ears.

Wanda's husband, Heath, an incredibly tall, well-muscled hunk of a man, reached a large hand out and cupped the baby's head with a sympathetic smile. He dropped a kiss on the top of his light brown head while wiping the tears from the baby's cheeks with his thumb.

"Buddy, what's the trouble? Daddy will do anything to make it better."

Baby Schwartz-Jefferson bowed his body with another ear-piercing howl, arching his spine out and away from Wanda, whose tears now flowed freely down her creamy cheeks.

Her lower lip trembled when she whisper-sobbed, "He hates me. Us. Everything. This was supposed to be a special day. A celebration. A day to welcome him into our family, and now..."

Keegan, yet another delicious specimen of paranormal male—and Marty's other half—shook his raven-haired head, squeezing Wanda's shoulder.

"Impossible, lady. You're the most likeable person I know, and this *is* a special day. It's just noisier than first anticipated. What's a party without some noise?"

Nina pushed her way past the men and held her arms out. "Okay, that's enough of that whiny BS, Wanda Jefferson. Give me the kid and you go get your shite together. Wash your face, brush your hair, moisturize, whatever. I'm not gonna to have you questioning the meaning of your existence because the kid's disoriented. Hand him over to Auntie Nina. Go find your center while I see if there's some kind of spell I can cast to help. Darnell," she called over her shoulder at the large man in gold high-tops who looked like a teddy bear dressed as a rapper. "Grease up those silky-smooth vocal chords, buddy. I feel a round of 'Wheels On The Bus' comin' on."

Darnell grimaced as his weary chocolate-brown eyes met Nina's. "I got you. Whatever y'all need, boss."

The stately, elderly gentleman named Archibald, with the kind blue eyes ensconced in a smiling face, dressed as though he'd come from the eighteen hundreds in his formal manservant wear, nodded and tugged at his throat. "Oh, Miss Nina, no more 'Wheels On The Bus'. I beg you—*beg you.* What say you to a rousing 'Michael Row The Boat Ashore'? I daresay, I'm a mean contributor when singing in the round."

Nina scooped up the screaming baby from Wanda and slapped Archibald on the back with a chuckle. "Been a rough few days, huh, buddy?"

His grin wore some frayed edges as he ran the back

of his hand over the baby's plump cheek, but still his gaze was filled with joy. "I daresay, 'tis been at the very least loud. I believe we've sung every song in the history of baby songs, to which our fair master has quite promptly turned his nose up. Yet, howling aside, we already love him as our own. Do we not, young sapling?"

"Sapling," Nina snorted, wrinkling her nose at Wanda as she made her way across the wide family room filled with beautiful Belgian farmhouse décor in a soft palette of creams and light sage greens, with stone pots full of lavender. "Can we get a name here, please, Mommy? Tell Mommy she needs to give you a name, Punkin'. How do you feel about Screech?"

The baby responded by batting his fists in the vampire's face.

"Okay. You don't like it. I'm not insulted. We're only making suggestions here," she replied, nibbling at his jaw, refusing to be deterred by his angry cries. She made another proposal as she whisked him off with Darnell and Archibald in tow. "Oh! I know. Mouth? Or Mouthy with a Y or maybe a double E? You know it's all the flippin' rage for new parents to turn a simple name into a spelling bee just to be different these days."

As if the poor child hadn't opened his mouth wide enough before, he did so this time by staring directly at the beautiful woman and literally screeching in her face.

Yet still, Nina wasn't put off. "And people complain

about how loud I am. Sheesh, buddy. Yer takin' my cake."

As Nina took the baby off to another room in Wanda and Heath's amazing house, and assorted offspring of the group played in the big farmhouse kitchen, Sally Brice—Sal, to the maybe two friends she had left—quietly observed from her corner in an overstuffed armchair while pretending to write notes on a legal pad.

As things quieted once more, Wanda finally ventured a sheepish peek at her and smiled an apology. "I'm so sorry you had to see us like this, Miss Brown. I find I'm so emotional these days. We weren't expecting... I mean, the agency didn't tell us to expect you today..."

Miss Brown. She had to remember she hadn't used her real name or she'd blow her cover.

Sal held up a hand and shook her head. "Not at all. But surprise home visits are a part of the package, I'm afraid." She patted herself on the back. That sounded very natural. Like she had a total clue as to what she was talking about.

Wanda—elegant, refined, utterly ruffled—folded her hands in her lap. "I guess we really surprised you with all the carrying on, huh?"

Sal had come here full of vim and vigor, ready to rip the baby from the arms of his new parents, only to be astounded by what greeted her. People. So many pretty people all packed into a room, doing everything in their cumulative power to stop this baby from a moment's unhappiness.

They soothed. They cajoled. They supported each other in an endless round of patience and understanding. After a half hour of all the screaming, Sal wanted to make a run for it, but she couldn't.

She wouldn't. She was mesmerized by this network of men and woman known as OOPS and their unwavering devotion to each other and the comfort of this child.

Sal didn't like it. Or rather, she didn't want to like it, but even she had to admit the baby was in good hands. But that didn't give her any explanations. She wasn't here to be wooed. She was here for answers.

So instead, Sal played the part she'd come to play. Social worker—which was a huge stretch for someone as ridiculously inexperienced with kids as she was.

Searching her mind, Sal tried to recall the million and two movies she'd seen featuring infants and the advice she knew had to be stored somewhere in her head.

Taking a deep breath in the silence that had enveloped the family room, with its comfortable furniture, throw pillows and blankets in muted blues, creams and white, she took a stab at it.

Leaning forward, Sal tucked her hair behind her ear into the conservative bun at the back of her head. "You know, I think your friends are right when they say he just needs to adjust. It's true. He can sense a new environment, new crib, etcetera, and that may take him a bit to warm up to. Babies like yours, who've been in an orphanage for a time, can sometimes react adversely to the love I'm certain you want to shower on him. He's not used to being kissed and hugged. Cuddling and playtime and all the things crucial to a baby's development sometimes go by the wayside in favor of just getting the job done. While the orphanage takes great pride in providing all the necessary things like food and shelter, they're strapped for the equally important hugs and kisses and say...er...tummy time."

Phew. Where she'd pulled the phrase "tummy time" from was a mystery, but they all appeared to absorb the information and nod as though she made sense—which was an enormous relief.

Marty's finger shot up in the air, her blue eyes twinkling. "Tummy time! Right. That helps strengthen his shoulders and neck, yes? But he should always be supervised, if I recall. It's been so long since Hollis was born, I've forgotten."

Wanda sat up straight and smoothed her flowing floral skirt over her thighs. "I don't think tummy time is what he's so upset about, but I'll try anything to get him to calm down. This can't be good for him. I can't bear to see him so unhappy. I know it's a million times worse for him, but... It's..."

"Upsetting," Sal finished for her, crossing her ankles, only to catch a glimpse of her ugly, brown orthopedic shoes. Buying them had seemed to make perfect sense. They felt like something a social worker would wear when she was trying to come off stern and authoritative. Now, in front of all these pretty people, she just felt foolish. "I can only imagine how hard this has been for you as a new mother. Adoption has a way of throwing you into the burning ring of fire, doesn't it?"

But Wanda waved a slender hand at her. "No, no! Forget about me and how I feel. I'm sorry you had to see me cry. I'm not normally so emotionally overwrought. You'd think I'd actually birthed the baby and was suffering from post-partum from the swing of my hormones. Anyway, it's not me we need to worry about. It's him. I want him to feel safe, loved, comfortable. We waited a long time for him. I'm determined to do this right, and seeing him cry like this is tearing me apart."

Sal's heart clenched into a tight ball. Samantha would have loved to hear Wanda was so invested.

Pretending to write something on her legal pad, she smiled at the lovely woman again. "How long ago did you apply with the agency to adopt?"

Heath smiled, twin grooves appearing on either side of his mouth. His classically handsome features beamed with pleasure. "Last October. We thought it would take forever to be approved, but as you know, we have forever to wait," he joked.

Wanda actually chuckled and smiled up at her husband, who'd come to crouch beside her rocking chair. She tugged at the collar on his fitted shirt in a loving gesture. "It's true. We do have an eternity."

Sal couldn't help but let a smile slip, too. "You're

both...?" she asked, a leading tone in her question because she didn't know their species.

"Vampires," they chimed in simultaneously, then laughed. "Well, I'm half werewolf, half vampire." Wanda smiled again, her face bright, her skin creamy smooth.

"How interesting. Bet that's some story, huh?" Sal couldn't help but be fascinated by these people she wanted to hate. They were all so...so...nice.

Now Marty, snugly fitted against her husband's side, chuckled. "If you only knew the things we've all been through."

The one thing Sal *did* know was what they'd been through. She knew people all over the globe. She heard the gossip in their paranormal world. In and amongst their kind, these women in particular were legend. "So I've heard. I know all about OOPS."

Wanda's face instantly went worried and she was quick to reassure. "But we're very careful when we accept a client at OOPS. I mostly do a lot of soothing and comforting. Nina's the muscle of our group. I promise you, I try and stay as safe as possible."

But Sal shook her head and held up a hand. "That's not why I'm here, Mrs. Jefferson. I'm only here to check on the baby's well-being and observe. Not to judge your chosen path in life."

Though, the whole OOPS support group thing did worry her, if she were honest. These women saved all sorts of people from paranormal crisis. Often, the clients they dealt with were in an accidental predicament. The women swooped in, at no cost to the client, and selflessly put themselves on the line to help them learn to adjust to their new lives.

If what she'd heard were true, some of the stories were incredible—and dangerous. Who'd take care of the baby if something happened to Wanda? Though, Sal already knew she had the answers. They were all right in this room. They were singing songs to soothe an irate baby in the *other* room. The baby would never want for a thing with this bunch.

That left her comforted. But that also left Sal deflated. Still with plenty of unanswered questions, but deflated.

Rising, Sal ran a hand over her hair then held it out to Wanda, who rose instantly, too, and enveloped her fingers with a warm grip.

"Again, I'm sorry your visit was so…loud. Please feel free to drop by anytime."

Sal almost winced as she let go of Wanda's hand. This was her last connection to Baby Schwartz-Jefferson, and it was slipping away as quickly as sand in an hourglass.

Fighting the threat of tears, she composed herself enough to ask, "Might I make a suggestion to help with the baby's care?"

Wanda's face relaxed a little, making it clear she was open to contributions. "Anything, of course. *Please.*"

"I know you'll find this unconventional, or maybe even a little crazy. I also know the adoption agency will tell you if you allow the baby's human side to take over, he'll eventually stop crying. But I can't bear to hear his cries either. And it isn't like you can explain to him the craving will pass like you might with an adult."

Wanda's head tilted to the side. "*The craving*? The agency didn't say anything about cravings. They said he just cries sometimes. They actually said to let him cry a little longer each time before rushing in to soothe him. They told us to just ride it out and it would pass. But they didn't explain much else. Though, his crying surely hasn't passed, so I'm not sure what you mean by cravings."

Yeah. She'd bet that's what they told her. Naturally, they hadn't told her the most important bit about adopting this baby because it wasn't exactly pleasant—or even terribly legal.

"That's all well and good, and eventually, I'm positive you'll be able to wean him, but for now and up to the first year, his development is crucial."

Wanda frowned. "Wean him? I don't understand, but just tell us what we need to do. *Please.*"

"For the love of Popsicles, pleeeaase tell us!" Nina shouted from another part of the house, where the baby's muffled cries continued as another round of "Michael Row The Boat Ashore" began.

"I'm sorry, I've gotten ahead of myself with words like cravings and weaning. Here's what I mean. He needs brains, Mrs. Jefferson. A baby zombie needs brains."

CHAPTER 2

Wanda's mouth dropped open, but Marty rushed in to speak for her friend. "Brains? Like, the morgue and dead people and well, you know...dead people?"

Sal nodded her head as she made her way to the cheerfully antiqued double doors, preparing to leave. "I do know. I also know the council and all their hags combined wouldn't know how to deal with a zombie baby any more than they know how to deal with *me*—a banshee. Banshees are rare, too."

"A banshee? What in the name of Twinkies is a banshee?" Nina yelped. "Knew you smelled weird!"

"Can it, Elvira!" Marty shouted to her. "Please, continue, Miss Brown.

Sal hid another smile. This Nina was really something. "Anyway, I'm sure they'd like your baby to integrate into the human world just like everyone else, and in some instances, I agree. We can't have everyone running around willy-nilly, eating livestock or drinking blood from innocents—"

"Whoever made that rule is a moron!" Nina called out over the baby's cries.

Sal almost laughed, but instead, she nodded her head in a sage bounce. "My point is, there are maybe four or five zombies in the world at large. Your baby is rare—so rare. But he's only half human, and I have it on good authority he needs brains to quell his cravings. I can't think of a single really good reason why the council prevents you from collecting a brain or two—the person you'd take it from is, after all, dead and won't miss it. Yes, science could surely use it, I suppose, but in the face of allowing a baby to suffer, I don't see the harm. However, the council's all about being as politically correct as possible, and that means letting your baby suffer while he waits for his human half to take over. Council calls it a *process*. I call it baloney."

"Brains? Process?" Wanda repeated, her gaze far away. "My God, it all makes sense. We're so used to Carl—who happens to be the product of a very tragic accident, by the way—and his broccoli, I guess it just never occurred to us. I feel so stupid!"

"Carl?" She'd wondered about Carl ever since she saw his name on one of her reports. How did a zombie survive on broccoli alone? Never mind that, how did Carl survive when all his organs were dead? The mysteries of the paranormal would never cease to amaze her.

Marty nodded and smiled. "Yes. Didn't you read

about him in the intent-to-adopt statement Wanda and Heath wrote?"

Shit. No. She hadn't because, well, she was a big fat liar right now. Refusing to become flustered, Sal improvised while giving them a weary look. "I deal with so many cases. It must've slipped my recollection of the case."

"I'm sure you're busy," Marty soothed. "Anyway, Carl lives with Nina, but he's family to all of us. He's a fully-grown adult who suffered a spell gone sideways via a witch doctor. We found him while we were on a case. That was Harry's case, right?" She looked to Wanda for confirmation.

Wanda agreed with her friend. "Yes. That was a doozy."

"Harry?" Sal asked, though she knew she shouldn't muddy the waters further.

Marty smiled her sunshiney smile. "He's my sister-in-law's husband. I can't explain how Carl ended up not needing brains the way zombies do, but he loves broccoli and almost any vegetable—he's almost totally vegan. He speaks in one-word sentences most times, and that's after Nina spent countless hours teaching him how. And he reads, too. Anything and everything. He loses digits we have to duct-tape back onto his hands on the reg, but has a heart the size of half the eastern hemisphere, and he's truly a treasure. Still, he'd never survive without Nina. I don't even know if he knows he's supposed to eat brains. In fact, I'm pretty sure he doesn't even know he's a zombie."

"Is he half human, too?" Sal asked, intrigued. Samantha would have liked to have met someone like her—even if he couldn't speak.

Heath shrugged his wide shoulders, reaching for Wanda's hand to tuck it against his side. "We don't know for certain. We only suspect. Whatever happened to him when that witch doctor Guido tried to change him back with some hinky spell he'd concocted, it got royally screwed up, and Carl is the product of some poorly executed magic. But he definitely doesn't eat brains."

Sal looked around the spacious room with its enormous potted plants and pictures of friends and family. "Where is this Carl?"

"With his aunt Teddy on her ranch in Colorado," Nina called out over the now weakening cries of the baby.

Wanda bobbed her head. "She has an exotic animal rescue and our Carl loves animals. Nina tries to expose him to all sorts of things—different environments, people and so on. So when our friend Teddy called to see if he'd like to come out for a week of horseback riding and hanging out with her husband Cormac, Nina, nervous Nellie that she is, actually consented. He'll be back tomorrow."

That, too, reassured Sal the baby would at least have some exposure to where he came from. Sort of.

"Did they give him brains at the orphanage? How could they have possibly allowed him to cry for an entire month?" Wanda asked, threading the fingers of her free hand together in a nervous gesture.

Sal's stomach plunged in a downward spiral. "I don't know, Mrs. Jefferson. I do know the cravings for brains don't always start at birth. I don't even know how he came to be at the orphanage, truthfully. They don't give me that information. I'm the aftercare, so to speak. You went through an adoption agency, didn't you? To adopt him?"

Heath nodded, tightening his grip on Wanda's hand. "We did, and we gave a sizeable donation for expenses for the mother and whatever else was needed, of course. It was our understanding the agency had no history on the baby. The only information they gave us was the little guy was in an orphanage until they matched him with us. They felt it was best to keep his adoption closed and we agreed to do that until he's eighteen. Then I believe he has the right to know where he came from if he so wishes."

The agency. Sal had to fight not to roll her eyes. That damn Bright Futures Paranormal Adoption Agency was a joke. She just didn't know how much of a joke, or why these nice people were mixed up with a place like that. So she hid her disgust.

"So no prior history..." Sal muttered and reached for the door handle. "I'm sorry. I wish I could help more. The only thing I can tell you for sure is your baby needs brains."

"Uh, nice social worker lady?" Nina interrupted as

she came from the back of the house back into the living room. "Any big ideas on where to get the brains?"

Oh, sure. She had plenty of ideas. In fact, when she left here, she was going to go heist some and drop them on Wanda's doorstep. But would a reputable social worker know sketchy info like that? Likely not.

"I'm sorry, Mrs. Statleon. I don't know specifics. I only know what I've heard in my many years of experience as a...social worker."

Wanda held her hand out again, her eyes weary. "You've done plenty. We'll figure it out from here. Thank you, Miss Brown. I hope the next time you see us, it will be under much quieter circumstances."

"Thank *you*, Mrs. Jefferson. Both of you," Sal said, acknowledging Heath as well. "Much luck and happiness with your new family."

As she stepped out into the bright sunshine of a May day, it was all Sal could do not to run right back in there and yank the baby from their arms just to keep her attachment to Samantha as close as possible.

It didn't matter that she didn't know thing one about caring for a baby. Her life was her own and she liked it that way, but for Samantha? She'd do anything. Even raise a baby.

That included pretending to be a social worker—which she felt rather confident she'd pulled off as she raced down the wide front porch steps of the Jeffersons' gorgeous home, carefully avoiding planters overflowing with spring flowers. Rounding the corner of the street, she began pulling off her demure jacket in shades of a dull brown that matched her equally demure skirt and pulled the pins from her hair to let it flow down her back.

Pausing for a moment, listening to the sounds of a quiet Saturday afternoon in suburbia, she gulped in deep breaths. As sprinklers chugged and lawnmowers mowed, she swiped at the tears falling down her face with impatient fingers. Tears for the loss of Samantha. Tears for a life she'd never had—nor likely ever would.

Sal smiled when she saw her motorcycle, parked at the curb lining this beautiful street with its tall oak trees and well-maintained gardens full of bright geraniums and pansies. Riding would wash away her anxiety. At least for a little while.

Maybe she'd head toward the Poconos after she grabbed some brains for the baby. It was a beautiful day and the drive would do her good, maybe clear her mind.

As she prepared to sling her leg over the seat, hiking up her skirt to reveal biker shorts, someone grabbed her by the arm and squeezed.

"Are you goddamn well insane?"

Oh, good. The party-crashing skinwalker'd arrived. "Depends on who you ask, Private Detective."

In an instant, Grey Hamlin's face was blocking the buttery ball of sun, darkening her day. "Didn't I tell you after you literally stole the info I had on those people you had to promise to stay the hell away from them?"

Sal yawned, leaning forward to grab her helmet

from her bike's handle as she shrugged him off. "And didn't I tell *you* not even Satan himself could prevent me from checking on the baby? Why would I take your word for anything?"

He planted his hands on his lean hips. "You're asking for trouble, Brice. I found the damn baby for you. The baby's fine. No. The baby's great. The baby lucked out. The baby hit the parental lottery and I told you that in good faith. Can't you leave well enough alone?"

Sal popped her lips as she made a thick braid of her hair, letting it drape over her shoulder. "You've known me for what—six months now? Surely you know 'well enough' isn't what I do."

Grey huffed a breath and glared down at her with his gorgeous green eyes. "You hired me to do a job and I did it. I gave you the pictures. His birth certificate—everything. That should have damn well been enough."

God, Grey was sexy. Still just as sexy as the day she'd gone to him and offered him all the money and information she had in the world to help find her best friend Samantha Carter. "Then why do you give a rat's ass what I do now that your job's done? Check cleared, didn't it?"

His hard jaw went harder, the stubble lining it dark and prickly. "Call me crazy, but I don't want to see you get hurt."

"Hurt? How the hell can I get hurt and why are you following me around like some whipped puppy?"

Hurt. He had some nerve talking about hurt after he'd broken up with her. *That* had hurt.

He clamped his yummy lips shut for a moment, but then he smiled his gorgeous smile, flashing those perfect teeth he'd once told her his parents paid big bucks for.

"First, isn't seeing the baby of your best friend, your last link to her, hurtful? Because you can't tell those nice people in there who you are. The deal was if I found him, you'd shut your mouth about how you found him because it can cause me all manner of grief."

He was right. That had been the deal. But she refused to acknowledge as much out loud. Instead, she lifted her chin and averted her gaze, focusing on a lovely row of holly hedges.

But Grey tipped her chin up with a finger and forced her to see him. "Second, I rather think of myself as more sensei than puppy. You know, guiding you. Sort of wax-on, wax-off style," he quipped. Which was just like Grey. When he didn't want to talk about his emotions, he resorted to jokes.

She revved the engine of her bike, making sure it was nice and loud, then pulled her body away from his luscious one. "Well, listen up, Mr. Miyagi. You made it clear as day we were over. And that's fine. You did your job and you washed your hands of me. In my mind, 'over' means you no longer trail behind me like stale breadcrumbs and go your merry way while I go mine. So what's wrong? Is your way not so merry? Do ya miss me, Grey? Isum's wonewee?" she taunted, because it felt good to lash out.

Because damn him to hell, she missed him with an ache she'd only felt once before in her life. When her best friend went missing. But the hell she'd let Grey Hamlin see that. The hell she'd let him know the smell of his cologne was killing her right now.

Or that the feel of his fingers around her arm sent wave after wave of tingles along her skin—or even that his perfect body, with all its angles and edges, didn't even have to be touching hers to leave its imprint.

The hell.

She'd made a stupid mistake when she'd fallen for the guy she'd hired out of desperation. Private Detective Grey Hamlin, in all his dark, mysterious smexyiness, had sucked her in and spit her back out once the job was done. He was right. He had done what she'd paid him to do.

Found her friend and then later, when she'd learned Samantha had a baby, she'd asked him to find the baby, too.

And he'd done that.

He'd also dumped her the moment he'd located the baby.

Morphing into an exact replica of her, as skinwalkers are wont to do, Grey made a big deal of tossing his hair just like she did and mocked, "Isum's is not at all lonely. Isum's is perfectly fine, thank you. And FYI, I miss you like I'd miss a good bout of the bubonic plague."

God, she hated when he did that. At first, his ability to morph into virtually anyone after seeing them only once had freaked her out. She'd never met a skinwalker in all her thirty years, but her research had told her they only turned into animals.

However, Grey, like her, was considered highly evolved, and could turn into most anything or anyone with just a glance at their behaviors. He didn't even need to touch them. The trouble, or at least he said it was troubling, was he couldn't do it for long.

After she'd gotten used to it, and understood it only made him a better detective to have that kind of power, it became a laugh riot when he morphed into someone. When they'd been together and the laughs were aplenty, that is. But his skinwalking abilities weren't nearly as funny now that she was his target.

"Isum's can fuck off," Sal responded, flipping him… er, herself the bird.

God, that was weird.

He morphed back and pulled his reflective sunglasses off the top of his head, placing them on his nose. You know, so she couldn't see whatever it was he was hiding in those green-green eyes.

Running a hand over his thick dark hair, he jammed them into the pockets of his tight jeans. "And I'll do just that as soon as you're on your way.

"What the hell are you doing here anyway? What is it that you want from me, Grey? Go away."

He clucked his tongue in clear admonishment. "I want you to promise me you'll leave the Jeffersons alone and let them raise that baby. They're good people. Honest people. Besides, I can't afford for people like them, important people in our world, to know I helped you hunt them down. They're influential in our world, Sal. They have a ton of respect from the council. I don't need the big guys trampling my little corner of the universe."

Tears burned the back of her eyelids. Baby Schwartz-Jefferson was the last link she had to her best friend. She knew leaving him and his new family in peace was the right thing to do—her brain knew, that is. Her heart? Her heart wanted to snuggle him against her cheek and inhale his scent, see if his eyes were like Samantha's, or if he had any of her traits at all.

And if she promised Grey she'd leave the Jeffersons alone, did that mean he'd leave *her* alone? Forever? Did it mean he'd stop popping up in her life? Maybe, even if the attention was negative, she *wanted* him to keep popping up in her life.

Which is pathetic, Sal. Epically pathetic.

Straightening her shoulders, she decided she agreed with her inner voice and it was time to cut the cord. "Fine. I promise to leave them alone. Heaven forbid I should screw up your shady little detective business. We done?"

He paused a moment, almost as if he wasn't done. But then he let her arm go and backed away from the bike, holding up his wide hands like white flags. "Done."

Flipping a hand up as though she didn't care a lick,

Sal waved him off in dismissal. "Sayonara, Hamlin," she called before taking off down the perfectly paved street with the perfect houses and perfect yards to head home to nothing once more.

Absolutely nothing.

~

Grey ran a hand over his hair again, sighing a ragged breath as he watched Sal turn into a dot on the horizon, her hair flying in an inky black ribbon from beneath her helmet. That damn woman was going to be the death of him. She was like keeping a grip on a greased cat, but if she didn't watch her pretty ass, she'd stick her nose in something she had no way to protect herself from.

And all because she just wouldn't let shit go.

When she'd come to him for help a few months back, he'd been prepared well in advance. Carefully placed informants ensured Sal Brice would hear about him when she flew onto his radar, asking questions about the disappearance of her best friend Samantha Carter.

Samantha was half human, half zombie—a very rare combination in the world of paranormals and highly prized. When she'd gone missing, no one paid much attention until her name became associated with something much bigger than just her disappearance.

So Sal, asking around about her, sent up red flags. She'd done just as he'd hoped she would and sought his "private detective" help. In order to contain the little firecracker and keep her from screwing up months of hard work, he'd taken her case in the hopes he'd give her a trickle of information and she'd move along.

In the end, that was all part of the bigger picture. What wasn't part of the bigger picture was how strongly drawn to her he'd been. Like, insanely drawn to her, and she to him.

Yet, things changed further when she'd come to him midway into the investigation and told him about her vision of Samantha's death and the mention of the baby. It changed everything, which meant he had to bail from their relationship, and bail fast, so he'd improvised and revised the whole plan by finding the baby for her.

But the plan hadn't included falling in love with Sal Brice. He'd done everything he could to prevent it. He'd ignored the tingle in his chest whenever she'd shown up with one of her crazy leads on Samantha's whereabouts.

He'd ignored her plump lips, her sexy scent, her long, straight black hair. He'd fought to keep her safe while she'd stomped her way through lead after lead like an elephant on a rampage.

He'd tried like hell to resist her—even if her dedication and loyalty left him in awe.

And Jesus, he'd failed miserably. So he'd broke it off before it got any worse and she caught on to his game.

Seeing her today had killed him, but letting her go

was the smartest thing he could do if he wanted to keep her safe. It really was the only way.

Now, he just hoped she'd do as promised and keep her nose out of things.

And then he remembered whom he was dealing with and sighed again.

CHAPTER 3

Sal was just about to drop off the cooler of brains, complete with instructions for the Jefferson's, when the front light on their porch switched on, flashing a bright beam in her eyes.

Oh, to have Grey's skinwalking abilities now.

"Mind telling me what the fuck you're doing out here, Social Worker Brown?"

Standing up straight, Sal brushed the thighs of her leather pants with sweaty palms. "Surprise home visit?" she squeaked, licking her suddenly dry lips.

Nina, the looming vampire, crossed her arms over the chest of her black hoodie and sucked her cheeks inward.

Wow, she was stunning.

Even caught red-handed, Sal could appreciate her beauty. If you had to look like someone, it wasn't a bad gig to look like Nina for an eternity.

Using one finger, Nina wrapped it under the lapel

of Sal's leather jacket and hauled her upward, leaving her legs to dangle. One finger. She was using *one finger* to hold up all of Sal's weight—which was by no means feather-ish.

"At midnight?"

Okay, so it had taken her longer than anticipated to break into a morgue and get the brains, a disgusting job if ever there was one, but it hadn't been the in-and-out job she'd hoped. So she was running late. Plus, she'd been bogged down by her run-in with Grey and all the emotions the encounter evoked.

Swallowing, Sal looked into Nina's swirling black eyes, now narrowed and angry. "That's why it's a surprise?"

Nina's nostrils flared as she appeared to sniff Sal. "*Bullshit.*"

Her eyes flew open wide even as her heart thrashed against her ribs. This was a vampire, and a badass one at that, according to the reports she'd read.

"Noooo. No, no. Not bullshit. It's not a surprise if I tell you I'm coming," she defended. It was a weak defense, and it came out kind of wimpy, but it was all she had.

"Who the fuck are you? You've got exactly five seconds to spit it out or I *rip* something out. From your body. Ready? Set. Goooooo!" Nina roared in her face.

As Sal's legs swung beneath her and she flailed helplessly, her mind raced for the facts of her cover story she'd repeated to her reflection over and over until she had it right. "I already told you. I'm Sabrina Brown and

I work for Bright Futures Paranormal Adoption Agency. I'm a social worker there."

"Again, I call bullshit. Before you asked if Wanda went through an adoption agency to adopt the kid, didn't you? Now you work for the adoption agency she adopted the kid through? Which is it?"

Oh. Shit. Had she said that? Oops.

She swallowed and stared Nina right in the eye. "I'm new there. Sometimes I forget things..." *Or I forget which lie I told. Whatever.*

"Yeah, right," Nina drawled. "So what's it gonna be, *Sabrina Brown*? You wanna start with your intestines or are your eyeballs dying for a peek at the inside of your brain?"

Somehow, Sal knew this wasn't some idle threat. She'd heard about Nina and her role in OOPS. Hell, Wanda herself admitted she was the muscle of the group. Judging from her body language and the glare Nina was giving her, she decided to trust the information was correct.

Gripping Nina's wrist, she cried out, "Wait! Let me explain. Please!"

"Nina!" Marty's face appeared from behind the vampire, her eyes wide. "What the frack are you doing to Miss Brown? Put her down now, you heathen!"

Wanda wasn't far behind Marty as she poked her head out of the doorway, the faint cries of the baby coming from the background. "Nina! Oh, my God! You put Miss Brown down now or I promise you, young lady, I'm going to—" She stopped mid-sentence and glanced guiltily at Sal. Smoothing a hand over her pretty lavender silk bathrobe, she squared her shoulders and appeared to compose herself. Clearing her throat, she said with a stern, matronly tone, "If you don't knock it off, I'm going to give you a good what for. It'll be the quiet corner for you and some serious time out, missy. Now put Miss Brown down. This instant!"

Nina reluctantly set Sal down on the front porch with a hard drop right next to a pot overflowing with red geraniums, pink Shasta, and purple pansies. But she didn't stop staring Sal down. "Okay. There. She's down. Now, care to tell me why Miss Brown's here at fucking midnight, Wanda?"

Suddenly, Wanda looked startled. "I don't know, but that's certainly no reason for you to manhandle her or use such foul language. I promise you, Miss Brown, Nina's very careful with her language around the children."

"So why are you here anyway, Miss Brown?" Marty asked, her eyes curious.

Damn, these people were still here. At midnight. The depth of their support took her breath away. Even though they had families of their own, and probably very full lives, they were here for Wanda. To help her get through this tough transition. Samantha had been that way, too. Ride or die. No matter what.

Sal inched backward, away from angry Nina, and felt around for the cooler. Pulling it to her chest, she held it out to them as though it were a peace offering. "Brains."

Aside from Nina, both women blinked. Nina, on the other hand, planted her hands on her hips and returned to her defensive stance and cynical gaze.

Sal swallowed, hoping to ease her dry throat. "I knew you'd need them. I know the baby needs them. There should be enough to last at least a month."

"And you, a *social worker,* knew where to get that shit? You got an in at the morgue?" Nina crowed. "If you're a social worker, I'm GD Miss America."

Marty snorted and tugged a length of Nina's shiny hair. "With these fried ends? As if."

Nina swatted her away with an angry hand full of fingers Sal was sure she wanted to wrap around her neck. "Shut that trap, Marty. Miss Brown's no damn social worker. What kind of social worker rides a Harley, wears leather, and has access to brains? That is your Harley, isn't it, *Miss Brown*?"

Straightening her shoulders, Sal pretended offense. "Are you saying social workers aren't allowed to have hobbies? That we can't enjoy a good hog because we deal with the welfare of children? Doesn't that come off a little like motorcycle-shaming?"

"Slow your roll, and save the competitive victim crap and kitschy millennial catchphrases for someone who gives a shite about your teeny-tiny feelings, lady. I said no such effin' thing. What I said was, you're full of shit and I'm onto you. In fact, maybe we should give that adoption agency a little ring-a-ling and ask them about you. Whaddya say, Hog Lover?"

Wanda grabbed at her friend's arm and swung her around to make eye contact. "Nina! Stop being so rude. Miss Brown did us a favor by bringing us brains, for pity's sake. I repeat—*brains*. You don't suppose she can get into trouble for that, do you? Of course she can! She took a risk to help us, which is more than I can say for the adoption agency that fed us a bunch of hogwash about adjustments and transitions. No offense, of course, Miss Brown."

Sal held up both her hands and smiled, avoiding Nina's piercing gaze for fear she'd set her on fire. "None taken."

Wanda let go of Nina's arm, but that disappointed teacher look never left her face. "I'm sure they were just following council's advice. Now, my poor son's been intermittently crying up a storm for hours and hours. I'm exhausted. We're all exhausted. If Miss Brown brought us something she shouldn't have, ask me if I give a flip. If someone told me he needed a Porterhouse with a side of fries and a light ale, you can bet your sweet vampire tuchas I'd put it in a blender for him. How can you be so rude to someone who so obviously went out of her way to help him—to help *us*? Now, apologize. Please." She waved a hand in Sal's general direction.

Aw, hell no. No apology necessary. Grey had been right to advise her to keep her nose out of things—because wow.

"Nope," Sal was quick to assure. "No need for apologies. I'm glad you have friends who look out for you, Mrs. Jefferson. Friends are so important."

"Friends who can smell bullshit," Nina muttered, but Marty jabbed her in the ribs with her elbow and frowned.

"Get in this house before I give you the beating you so richly deserve. And grab those brains. Let's figure out how to get them into the poor child before he wakes up and starts screaming again. Move it, Vampire." Marty pointed to the interior of the house and Nina went, but not before she used two fingers and pointed them first at her eyes then directly at Sal's.

"I see you, Social Worker. Remember that. I don't know what you're up to, but I'm gonna find out. Trust and believe," she warned, her tone sinister.

Wanda gave Nina a last dour look before Nina grabbed the cooler and headed back inside. She looked to Sal with pleading eyes. "I'm so sorry, Miss Brown. Nina's...well, she's always on guard. In some cases, okay, in most cases, she goes too far. But it's really out of love and her wish to keep us all safe. I promise you, she has a gooey inside."

Sal smiled, even if her heart ached. Nobody could appreciate a friend looking out for a friend more than she could. "I get it, Mrs. Jefferson. I genuinely do. I hope the brains help, but I need to get going now. It really is terribly late and I have...lots of children to check on tomorrow. So, have a good evening."

Clearly on impulse, Wanda reached for her, giving

her a quick hug and whispering tearfully, "Thank you. From the bottom of my heart, thank you."

And though the contact was brief, it smelled of cinnamon apples and sunshine and the scent lingered in Sal's nose, making her yearn for one last moment with Samantha. The only family she'd ever had.

She turned and ran down the steps as though the hounds of hell chased her so no one would see her cry.

Damn. Every time she turned up at the Jeffersons' she turned into an absolute mess, and Grey was right again. It had to stop. There was no way she could emotionally handle seeing Samantha's baby and not want to stick her two cents where it didn't belong. There was no way she could keep from telling them all the dreams Samantha had shared with her about the time when she created a family of her own.

Now that they had the brains, Sal had to walk away. He wouldn't suffer withdrawal. He wasn't alone in some row of cribs at some rundown orphanage where only his very basic needs were cared for.

He was loved. He would always be loved. He'd be protected and coddled all his life.

Sucking in the cool night air, she reached her bike and gripped a handle for support, letting her head fall forward and her back arch. Losing Samantha had been like an empty hole she just couldn't fill. Finding out why she'd disappeared had filled her days and nights for some time now.

But what was next? Where did she go from here?

What would fill her days and nights if she couldn't hash out the next move to finding the baby?

The future was an empty void of nothing but her and her dog, Buttercup.

She still didn't know what had happened to Samantha—not the details anyway. Maybe she'd never know. She'd die trying to find out, but the most important part of finding out where she'd gone had led her to the baby, and for that much she'd always be grateful.

"Didn't I fucking just tell you to go home?" someone growled from behind. "You're itchin' to make me keep my promise to eat your intestines, aren't you?"

Sal froze in the spotlight of the streetlamp, her hands going clammy as she turned around to face Nina.

God, this woman was scary as hell. But Sal fought to keep her composure when she turned and said, "I am going home. Right now. See me get on my bike and ride off into the sunset. Er...night. Whatever. I'm going. Swear."

Nina's eyes glittered before she melted right before Sal's eyes and turned into Grey. A laughing Grey.

Flicking her fingers in the air, she wagged them in his face. "Goddamn you, Grey! Go away! Ooooh, I hate when you do that!"

He shook a finger at her and winked as he trapped her against her bike. "I thought I told you today to stay away from these people? You made me a promise, Sal. It's not nice to make promises you have no intention of keeping."

She rolled her eyes at him, attempting to make herself small so their bodies wouldn't touch. "I did not promise. I agreed. And I was only trying to help them, for Christ's sake. The baby's suffering. He needed brains. I didn't even plan on them finding out it was me who got them the brains. I was just going to ding-dong ditch 'em after I dropped the cooler, but that damned Amazonian vampire who looks like a cross between Adriana Lima and Paulina Porizkova caught me."

Grey whistled and widened his stance, leaning down to gaze at her. "She's not hard on the eye, I'll admit, but I did hear her threaten you. Hot and angry makes for a very sexy package. She's one tough lady, huh?"

Sal fought a snort. Yeah. "Is tough the word you use when someone threatens to eat your intestines? Psychotic seems more fitting. And why are you still following me, eavesdropping on all my conversations? Jesus. Don't you have someone else you need to dump?"

"Tsk-tsk," Grey chided, running his index finger under her chin. "Don't be bitter, Sal. It's not your best look, and again, I'm only protecting my interests. I told you I could get shit for this if anyone found out I located the baby for you. I didn't exactly come about the information honestly, and I'm not exactly well loved by the council for my PI work. If they knew I'd been digging around on some esteemed members they think quite highly of, it might piss them off."

Leaning back, Sal let the bike cradle the small of her

back. "Yeah, yeah. But you know, I've always wondered how you found out about the baby to begin with. Care to share that info? Maybe give me the name of an informant or two?"

His eyes went hard like ice chips. "Why, so you can go mess with their lives, too? Pretend to be someone else you're not? Not on your life, Sal—or should I call you *Miss Brown*?"

Instead of staying angry, she let her emotions get the better of her. Giving him her doe-eyed look, she ran a hand over his hard chest. "Tell me one thing, Grey. Just one. Do you know what happened to Samantha before she got pregnant? I mean before I saw the vision of her dying. Where was she when I first started looking for her? How did she end up pregnant to begin with?"

Grey's eyes glittered in the velvety black of the night, hard and unyielding. "You know I don't have the answer to that, Sal. The only information I have is that she ended up pregnant, then... Well, you know what happened then. Anyway, it was just like your vision told you. How that happened or with whom, I don't know."

Clenching her fists, she fought the knot in her throat. Nothing kept her up at night more than the vision she'd had of Samantha in some dark, dirty room, giving birth to a squalling baby on sheets covered in blood and filth.

Nothing.

The only vision equaling it was the one she'd had

right after Samantha had somehow found a way to call her and confirm she'd truly had a child. In the middle of the phone call, while Samantha had begged her to "save the baby," she'd witnessed her best friend's murder, and then blacked out.

There was nothing in the vision to indicate how she'd been killed or by whom. Nothing. In fact, Sal didn't even have a location to go on. She'd seen nothing to give her a clue as to where the death had occurred. There'd been just Samantha's screams and her in a puddle of blood on the floor and her gut telling her she'd been murdered.

Her visions always came at a price—the loss of hours or sometimes even a day or two. The blackouts always followed the banshees' death screams. She'd had enough of them over the years to know the visions didn't lie. She'd witnessed more death in her lifetime than ten people, and her visions were never wrong.

Never.

Sometimes she was able to prevent the death from a vision—sometimes not. With no leads on Samantha's whereabouts, there was no way to keep her from death.

That was how, with every fiber of her being, she knew Samantha really was dead. The tiny tentacles of their energies, so connected since they were children, were gone. Flatlined. But there was a tenuous thread to the baby—one Sal had held on to as she'd looked for him.

She'd known he was real—that he existed. *Knew it.*

And she'd been right. But where had Samantha been all that time before the baby? She needed to know.

Removing her hand from his chest, Sal scoffed. "Same old brick wall, aren't you, Grey?"

He smiled at her, his dark hair falling over his forehead. "I remain as consistent as always."

Staring up at him, Sal shook her head, refusing to give in to how difficult seeing him was for her. Still, her gut clenched and her pulse raced as she prepared to leave.

"I have to go," she whispered, knowing this could well be the last time she ever saw him.

The notion made her heart ache in agony, but really, there was nothing left to say. He remained close-mouthed about how he'd found all the information on Samantha, just like he'd been from the get-go, and he'd broken things off with her. What else was left?

But Grey cupped her cheek, surprising her with a rare tender gaze. "Sal, look. I know you miss Samantha, and you're only trying to do what you think is right. You want to stay connected to Samantha through the little one, but you can't without revealing who you are. The baby really is in good hands. The best hands ever. He's going to have an amazing life. If what you've told me about her is true, Samantha would love that."

Yeah. She would love that. Sal knew in her heart she would.

Still, letting go...

Swallowing hard, she nodded, fighting an onslaught of hot tears burning the backs of her eyelids. She didn't want to cry in front of him. "I know. I do know. I'll let go now. I'll stop coming around. This time I promise."

Grey stared at her for a good long minute as though he wasn't sure he could trust she'd stay away, but then he leaned forward and kissed the tip of her nose. "Be good to yourself, Sal. Wish things could have been different," he whispered before he sauntered down the road, his long legs eating up the sidewalk, got into his jalopy of a car, and drove away.

Biting the inside of her cheek, she clenched her eyes and her fists in unison to thwart the tears and listened to the silence of a suburban night.

The only sounds she heard were the crickets chirping and the harsh beat of her empty, broken heart.

She'd been alone most of her life with the exception of Samantha. Forming relationships as a banshee was difficult at best when you were afraid to get too close to someone for fear you'd have a vision of their death.

If you didn't let anyone in, you couldn't harbor the vision of someone's horrible demise and torture yourself over whether you should share the information, could you? Because what if you couldn't stop the tragedy? It was easier to keep most everyone at a distance.

Both orphans, she'd met Samantha in one foster home or another when they were eight, and somehow they'd managed to stay together in the system until they graduated high school and got an apartment together.

Samantha, as a half human/half zombie, was as rare

in the paranormal world as Sal. She didn't know where she'd come from any more than Sal knew who'd hatched her, and that had created a bond that remained unbroken—until Samantha disappeared as though she'd never existed.

They'd only had each other for just over twenty years. Both afraid to look too far outside of their friendship for acceptance from someone else because no one understood them better than they understood each other. No one understood how difficult it was to form an attachment to someone when you've been shuffled through the system better than they did.

Sure, there'd been boys as kids, and eventually men as adults, but no one either of them had really fallen hard enough for to take the risk of permanency—well, until Grey. With Grey, she'd considered a commitment. Brief as the idea had been, he'd put the kibosh on that anyway.

Yet something with Samantha had changed just before she'd disappeared, and as close as they were, her BFF began keeping secrets and behaving erratically. To put it bluntly, she'd been an ass until Sal finally confronted her.

The last time she'd seen Samantha, they'd had a fight because of that confrontation. An all-out, balls-to-the-wall argument like they'd never had before.

And then she was gone. Just like that.

And Sal was still trying to find a way to deal with that kind of abandonment—that kind of hurt from the only person in her life she'd loved like family.

Squeezing her eyes shut, she tried to block out the last angry encounter with Samantha, telling Sal to stop clinging to her like some pathetic loser and find a life of her own.

Now, there was nothing left but to do just that.

One last long glance around at the beautiful neighborhood, with its lavish houses and long driveways, left her sighing before she slung her leg over her bike and prepared to keep her promise to Grey.

Just as she positioned herself on the bike, the hard crack of something heavy sounded, sending shooting pain through the back of her skull, knocking her out cold.

CHAPTER 4

"I damn well told you the bitch was a fraud. But did anyone listen? Nah," Nina scoffed in fed-up disgust. "Why listen to the broad with the magical sense of smell? What the fuck does she know? She's just the muscle of the group—the bitch who keeps your asses from being flattened. Could she possibly know what in the ever-lovin' fuck she's talking about? Don't be ridiculous. She's just your thug."

"Do they call you their thug, Nina?" a male voice asked, teasing sympathy in his tone. It sounded like Heath, but Sal couldn't quite open her eyes yet to see—her head hurt too much.

"They call me all manner of things, Heathcliff Jefferson. All fucking manner. And it usually has to do with my hot temper and my strength. I'm so much more than a good right hook with a purty face and great hair," she said with a sarcastic snort.

"Mean girls, the lot of them, eh?" Heath asked on a laugh.

"Dude, if you only knew the half of it."

"Oh, hush, Elvira. We do not just consider you the muscle. You contribute in other ways. But a large percentage of that contribution is, indeed, muscle and plenty of threats," Wanda defended as Sal fought a groan.

Damn her head hurt. Pounded, in fact. Throbbed to the beat of her racing pulse, despite the ice pack dripping water on her head, but no way was she stirring. Nina terrified her. Playing possum was her best bet.

"Mistress Wanda, how may I assist? Surely more ice won't help? Shall I make some tea? Do banshees drink tea? What in all of heaven is a banshee, anyway? Surely I should know the answer to this, yet I find myself puzzled."

For sure that was Archibald, with his crisp British accent and soft, lyrical tone. Banshees did, in fact, drink tea. But she wasn't a tea drinker. It was black coffee or a vodka neat.

There was a cracking of knuckles before Nina said, "Aspirin. Bring her some aspirin. A lot of aspirin. The bitch is gonna need it when I knock the shit out of her."

Just as she'd been considering opening her eyes, Sal kept them closed and tried not to shrink in fear.

"Oh, Princess Thug, knock it off," Marty commented. "She hasn't even had the chance to explain to us what's going on. Now, if we discover she's up to no good, I'll hold her down while you knock the shit out of her. Until then, lay off."

"What Marty said," Wanda agreed softly.

"What's to explain? She's a shady bitch. I go outside to check and see if she's really gone, and I catch some dude, nailing her in the back of the head with a damn bat. He'd have smashed her brains in if I didn't catch him so off guard I slowed his roll. Took off like a bat out of hell. So you two sensitive snowflakes tell me, why is a social worker gettin' her ass beat in the middle of suburbia?"

Someone had tried to knock her out? So yeah. Why was she gettin' her ass beat in the middle of suburbia? *Who* wanted to beat her ass? What was going on?

"Surely there are angry parents of children who've been taken and placed in foster care, aren't there? I imagine social work can be, in fact, a fiercely dangerous profession. Maybe he was an angry parent who felt wronged by the system?"

How lovely that Archibald was taking up for her. No one took up for her. Not since Samantha had died, anyway.

But Nina had that handled. "Baloney, Arch. Dude wasn't paranormal. He was a human. Doesn't she allegedly do *paranormal* social work? I'm not buyin' it. She's just a shady bitch."

Small feet sank into her belly and wandered up along her chest until she heard a distinct sniff. "She doesn't smell shady. She smells like...wait, gimme a sec... Um, a day-old tuna sandwich, mouthwash, apple shampoo and conditioner, and...dog food."

"Thank Jesus, you cleared that shit up for us, Calamity. Look, you might not be able to smell it, but I can. She ain't right."

No. No, she wasn't right. And she was going to have to open her eyes and face the music at some point. Maybe if she just lie here on Wanda and Heath's big poofy couch with her eyes closed, she'd be able to concoct another story that would convince Nina she wasn't shady.

But no can do.

Nina sat down on the couch and shoved her over with a firm hand. "Stop playing possum, Social Worker, and sit your ass up before I eat your face off. Who the hell are you and what the hell do you want with us?"

The eating of the face. That sounded so ugly and very messy.

"You got three seconds, then I'm gonna turn your world inside out. One, two—"

"No!" Sal cried, her eyes popping open. Okay, she'd caved. So what? Did it make her weak? Maybe, but having your face eaten off couldn't be pleasant. "My eyes are open."

Nina grinned, beautiful yet still sinister. "Good. Now speak or die."

"All these choices," Sal joked as she looked up at this volatile woman.

But Nina's pale face with the incredible cheekbones

remained hard as she leaned in and flashed her fangs. "Who the fuck are you?"

Heath placed a hand on Nina's shoulder, giving it a good squeeze. "Nina, don't make me side with the mean girls now. Ease off and let her sit up, okay?"

Heath's deep, resonant voice almost reassured Sal she was safe as long as he was here. Almost.

But Nina did as he asked and pushed off, rising to loom over her—all loomy and angry.

Marty rushed in then, offering Sal a hand to help her sit up, which she took with great hesitance until their fingers made contact, and Marty tightened her grip momentarily before letting go.

Sal's head swam as she tried to adjust her eyes to the soft lamps and bring everyone hovering over her into focus. Wobbling, she placed both palms on the cushions to keep herself upright before glancing at a bunch of expectant eyes.

Nina crossed her arms over her chest, her lips a thin line. "Who are you?"

Much as she hated it, especially in front of Nina, tears stung her eyes again. "My name is Sally Brice, but most people call me Sal."

"Okey-doke, *Sal*," Nina sneered. "Why are you here? And don't give me some canned bullshit about social work or whatever. There was a scrawny-ass but hella-scrappy dude outside, lookin' to bash your head in before I showed up. What does he want?"

Sal shook her head and clenched her fists to her

side. "I swear on everything I have, I don't know who'd want to bash my head in. I swear that's true."

The black cat, who'd left her chest and now sat on the back of the couch, sniffed the air around her again. "Smells like she's giving us the straight up."

"Why are you here, Sal?" Wanda asked, her tone fraught with worry as she tucked herself against her husband.

"The baby…" she murmured, low and slow, clenching her eyes shut. How could she explain without outing Grey or looking like some kind of crazy stalker?

There was a heavy silence that she couldn't find words of reassurance to fill just yet. But instinctively, she knew what they were thinking. They were thinking she was the baby's biological mother and she was here to try to take him back.

"Are you the baby's birth mother?" Marty finally asked on a hard gulp, reaching for Wanda's hand and bringing it to her cheek as though preparing to comfort her friend if Sal's next words declared her statement true.

"Answer the damn question!" Nina hissed, stepping in front of Wanda in a protective manner.

But Sal could only shake her head as the tears she'd held back today came gushing from her eyes to race down her cheeks.

"Then *who* are you?" Heath asked, his kind concern now taking a much harder edge as his handsome face darkened.

Inhaling, she pushed her hair from her face and looked up at him. "The baby's mother was my best friend in the whole world—or ever, actually."

Wanda let loose a small gasp as she sat in the opposite chair across from the couch. "*Was* your best friend?"

Sal's nod was slow. "She's gone..." She cleared her throat and looked directly at Wanda. "Dead. She's dead."

Nina stood behind the chair and gripped Wanda's shoulder. "Which leads me right back to the first question I asked. Why the fuck are you here pretending to be a damn social worker?"

Shuddering, she attempted to keep her voice steady. "I know. I know it's wrong. I mean, I knew it was wrong to come here and pretend to be someone I'm not. But... Samantha was my best friend for over twenty years, and I had to be sure, for her sake as well as mine, the baby was safe. That's all this is. I swear."

Marty sucked in her cheeks and tucked her hair behind her ear. "Okay. I mostly get that. Though, wouldn't it have been better to just ring the doorbell and ask? It's not like his adoption is a secret. Everything was done legally and aboveboard. So why the covert operation?"

"Would you have been receptive to me had I just rung the doorbell? I was trying to help the baby by getting him some brains and Nina nearly killed me."

Nina made a face at her and waved her finger in a negative fashion. "Nah. Don't pull that shit. I didn't want to kick your ass until I knew you were full of shit. If you'd just been honest, none of this would have happened."

Taking a deeper breath, Sal shook her head again, swiping at her hot tears. "Either way, I just wanted to know he was safe and…and loved. The agency doesn't give out information about the adoptions, as I'm sure you know. But I had to see for myself. For Samantha's sake."

Wanda nodded, her eyes softer now. "Wait. Did you say his mother's name was Samantha?"

Sal slid to the end of the couch, gripping the material of the arm to keep the room from spinning. "It was. Is that something you want to know?"

For some reason, she'd figured they wouldn't want to know details. She'd read that some adoptive parents preferred a distance between the baby and the birth mother, and when she'd read that, it stuck. Sure, there were plenty of open adoptions, but there were others who were uncomfortable knowing anything other than general background details like health history and place of birth.

Wanda looked surprised as she leaned forward, folding her hands in her lap. "Surely you can't think we don't care about where he came from, Sal? Of course we want to know. Do you have any idea how grateful I am to Samantha? I'm sorry she's gone, but the truth of the matter is, her death gave me the opportunity to have a child of my own. I've wanted this all my life—to be a mother. I never thought it was possible. I hate that she died, but I'll never be anything but grateful to her. I want to know everything about her so I can tell our son who she was—so I can tell him where he came from."

She wanted to hate these people, as irrational as it was, but she couldn't. They were everything she wasn't, nor could ever be.

Yet more tears stung her eyes as she smiled at Wanda through a wet haze. "I'm not here to take the baby or anything. I promise you. I can barely take care of myself and my dog, let alone a baby. I just *needed to* see..."

Wanda smiled through her own tears and nodded her head. "I understand."

"Samantha would have loved you all. I'm sure of that."

Wanda reached for her hand and squeezed. "So you'll tell me about her sometime? Maybe we could have lunch? I don't want to intrude on your memories. It's obvious you loved her very much, but maybe you'd share some things about her with me? If it's not too painful? And of course, you're welcome to see him anytime you'd like. I'm sure he'd love to meet the woman who brought him brains."

Sal let her hold her hand for a moment, enjoying the strange and instant warmth and comfort it brought. No one could have ever prepared her for the kindness this woman was showing her—even after she'd lied about who she was.

She bit the inside of her cheek to keep from

outwardly sobbing. "I'm sorry I lied, Wanda. I was just so…"

"Afraid and worried. Of course you were, Sal. She was your best friend. If one of my best friends died and her baby was put up for adoption, I'd move heaven and earth to find the child. Please know, I understand. I truly do."

But Nina's skepticism remained. "Whoa there, Nellie. Hold the damn phone. How 'bout you tell us how you found the kid in the first place, Not Really A Social Worker? I wanna know where you got the information. That agency said they didn't know who the birth parents were. Somebody just dropped the kid off and left him at the orphanage. So how'd you find him, and how do you know he's your friend's kid to begin with?"

She gulped, knowing she'd have to relive her vision out loud in order to explain how she knew such intimate details.

"Nina, don't be rude! The woman just lost her best friend, for crap's sake," Marty scolded with a knobby knuckle to her friend's shoulder.

Jamming her hands inside her hoodie, Nina rolled her eyes in her friend's direction. "Yep, and then she showed up here all cloak and dagger. I smell fish in Denmark and they're rotten. If you guys wanna go on believing her, fine. But I'm not taking any chances that little guy's gonna end up hurt. He's one of us now, and he stays one of us."

"I have visions," Sal offered lamely, her throat tight

from fear.

"Visions? Did you have one where I caught you bullshitting us?" Nina asked, her tone dripping with sarcasm.

"Let me just explain. Please." She paused, waiting to see if anyone objected. When no one did, she continued. "I'm a...a banshee. We're pretty rare at this point in the evolution of man. Mostly, a banshee has visions of people's deaths. It's random and weird and it makes for very few friends in life, and it's not nearly as exciting as being say, *a vampire*. Which is why Samantha and I were so close, seeing as she was rare, too."

Marty tried to hide her gasp, but Sal understood her surprise—and what her next question would be. "Did you have a vision about your friend's death? Oh, I'm so sorry. How awful for you."

Wincing, she twisted her fingers together in a nervous gesture. "I did. Actually, I had two visions. But just before the vision of her death, I saw Samantha give birth. She called me shortly after that and begged me to 'save her baby.' That's how I know her baby... I mean, *your* baby is hers biologically, because he has a birthmark on his heel just like Samantha. He does, doesn't he?"

"He does," Heath agreed, his eyes piercing hers, his strong jaw tight.

"And you saw her die?" Marty asked on a gasp. "What were the circumstances surrounding her death? Was it natural or an accident? Why wasn't she in contact with you? Had you just lost touch? Where was the father?"

All valid questions, for which she decided to give truthful, yet not-too-detailed answers. "No, we hadn't lost touch; we shared an apartment and one day, she just disappeared. I don't know who the father of the baby is. I was hoping you might know. As to her death, I'm unclear as to what caused it."

Wanda's hand went to her slender throat. "Oh, Sal, how dreadful. But I can tell you, we were told the baby was abandoned. We have no information on either parent."

"But that still doesn't explain how you found the location of the kid, Sal," Nina crowed suspiciously. "So you had two visions. One where you saw your friend give birth and another of her death. But you'd have to have seen the adoption papers to know how to find out where Wanda lives. So what isn't Sal telling us?"

How was she going to get through this without giving up Grey? Without giving up herself? Even if he'd dumped her, and hurt her by doing so, she didn't want the wrath of the council on his doorstep, and she didn't want to admit to any more deceit than she already had.

The only reason she knew where the baby had landed was because she'd snuck a peek at the paperwork Grey had on him.

Licking her lips, she decided to fudge the truth; just enough to be plausible without having to totally lie. "I know people. Not-so-great people, I guess. They did a little detective work for me and led me to you."

Nina popped her lips and rocked back on her heels. "Where are these people, Sal? Is the dude who clunked you on the head one of those not-so-great fucking people?"

But Sal sat up straight, her spine rigid. "I swear to you, I don't know who that was or why anyone would clunk me on the head. Maybe it was just some guy who wanted to mug me?"

"Here in suburbia? In the middle of the street? Where the worst thing to happen was when the guy across the road stole his neighbor's snowball-throwing Santa to keep him from winning the Christmas lights contest? Naw. Try again, Sal," she taunted with a purposely belligerent tone.

Marty poked Nina in the arm and frowned. "It's obvious she doesn't know anything, Angela Lansbury. Lay off, already. You're making her nervous."

Nina narrowed her gaze directly at Sal. "Good. She *should* be nervous because she's full of shit. Sal knows some not-so-great people is about as vague as it gets, and I'm not buyin' it. How'd ya find the baby, Sal? What do you do for a living that puts you in contact with some not so great people?"

Sal wilted under Nina's gaze as sweat trickled between her breasts. She'd always considered herself pretty tough, growing up in the system like she had. Always dodging a bullet in one foster home after the next, but Jesus, this Nina made her feel like a shrinking violet.

The problem was, Nina was right. Sure, she knew

some unsavory people. She was a bartender in a dumpy dive in the dregs of Brooklyn, for shit's sake, but she didn't know the kind of people who'd help her latch onto information so sensitive.

Which made her wonder for the millionth time about Grey and how he'd found out where the baby'd landed. Was he really that good of a detective? His crappy, musty office in a basement in Brooklyn sure didn't tell that story.

But she was intent on protecting him. He wasn't a bad guy because he didn't want a commitment. He'd treated her pretty great in the few weeks they'd spent together, mostly in bed, but out of bed he'd been considerate and sweet, too. She certainly didn't want to see him get into trouble just because he didn't want to shack up for life. She wasn't that girl.

So, Sal decided to go vague. "I'm a bartender. All sorts of scumbags come into where I sling booze. Scam artists, money launderers, fraudulent I.D.s. You get the picture. If you have the cash, they'll do almost anything."

"Okaaay, if that's true, Sal," Nina drawled, "why the fuck did the dude who whacked you say, and I quote, 'Samantha told me you were a nosy bitch,' just before he tried to bash your brains in?"

Sal's eyes went wide. She didn't remember that at all. Not a word of it.

Holy shitballs.

CHAPTER 5

"Goddammit, Morsey! You swore to me you'd look out for her just in case Samantha ever mentioned Sal to the bastard. So how the fuck did this happen?" Grey yelled into his cell as he paced the hallway of Sal's apartment building, trying to figure out a way to get inside so he could take Buttercup out.

"Nuh-uh-uh, buddy," his longtime partner, Carr Morsey chastised. "Here's the real question. How did the motherfucker end up on the street where that baby now resides? More to the point, why was the woman you were so sure could help us with this bullshit there, too? What aren't you telling me, pal?"

That instantly cooled his heels. *You mean the part about how I basically located the baby, gave her some vague intel and she snooped through my shit and found out the rest because I was all doped up on a sex high? Thus, leading the guy who knocked Samantha up then stole her baby and left her for dead right to the baby's location, and to Sal, too?*

Shit, shit, shit. He should have never given Sal even a little information on the baby. But he couldn't help himself. He was nuts about her—walking away from her was almost as hard as seeing her sob-gulping tears when she'd had the vision of Samantha dying.

The only way to assuage his guilt about not telling her who he really was ended up being his validation. It was how he'd appeased his conscience about telling her where Samantha's baby had landed. She'd promised to keep what he had told her to herself.

He'd been foolish enough to believe her. But he'd underestimated her devotion to her friend. It had been a long time since he'd had any sort of ties that were fresh enough in his mind to remind him what it was to care for someone so deeply the way Sal did about Samantha—or even the way he did for Sal, for that matter.

He almost couldn't blame her for snooping through his stuff, and it was his own damn fault he hadn't locked up that intel.

So, he'd made a stupid rookie mistake—something he was not. Now, if his assumption was correct, the baby's biological father or someone associated with him was on the hunt, and Sal was his target.

Jesus, this woman would break him.

"Look, I thought she was out of the damn picture. I left my post because you said I could go grab a burger. I came back just in time to see the last bit of a scuffle and then he took off. I was so caught off guard, I totally lost him. If anyone should have known she'd show the hell back up, it should have been you. You did sleep with her," Morsey defended.

She'd played him again. When she'd ridden off and didn't return, he'd thought she'd done just as he'd asked and let everything go. Dammit. Every skill, every instinct he had went by the wayside with her.

"Hamlin? What the hell are you doin'? Quit wankin' off and pay attention. You need to get her the hell out of that house and back in Brooklyn where she belongs. I can't do it because she doesn't know me, but she's going to fuck up months of work, buddy, and I wouldn't want to be you if McCall gets wind of it."

"Is she *still* damn well inside?" What the hell was she doing in there anyway?

"Yeah, she is. They're making her tea, for Christ's sake. Like she's family or something. Are you sure these are the people who've taken on some pretty hefty opponents? They have a manservant, for shit's sake."

Grey almost laughed. They were definitely an eclectic assortment of paranormals. "I'm sure. They're legendary, according to all the reports I've read on them."

"Man, who'da thunk these bunch could be so pretty to look at but so deadly. Maybe we should hire the whole girl gang," he joked on a gruff laugh. "Now get the hell in there and get her, would you?"

"All right," he growled, leaning against the dimly lit hallway wall. "I'm on it." He clicked the phone off and stared at it for a few seconds, angry—at himself, at Sal, at Morsey and at McCall, their bigwig boss.

How the hell was he going to get her away from the Jeffersons and crew and keep her away? It was only because of that woman Nina that she'd narrowly escaped having her skull bashed in, according to Morsey—and he was betting the lot of them wanted answers about what she was doing prowling around their doorstep.

Sal wasn't a good enough liar to pull off playing a social worker—especially if she'd been hurt and disoriented. Which meant he had to go in after her.

But first he needed to get inside her place and grab Buttercup. It was time for her evening walk, and he'd bet she'd love a ride in the piece of crap he'd been driving around since this all began.

That he knew the dog's schedule made him cringe. He'd become too deeply involved with Sal and now he was losing all perspective.

Picking the lock of her door, he pushed his way inside to find Buttercup pacing the worn linoleum of Sal's tiny kitchen. The smell of her apartment, filled with her scent, made him inhale sharply with that irritating longing he'd developed since they'd broken up.

As Buttercup noted his presence, he was grateful she had the dog. Not only was she massive, but she was a good deterrent in a neighborhood as shitty as Sal's.

When she caught sight of him, she lunged, all four

paws, all one hundred pounds of pit bull mix, and licked his face, almost knocking him over.

Grabbing onto her front paws with one hand, he stroked her wide head with the other and grinned. "Buttercup! Easy, sweetheart. It's good to see you, too, Cupcake. Did mommy leave you here all alone? Is it time for a walk and some dinner?"

The dog dropped down and ran for her leash, hanging by the door, her nub of a tail wagging happily on her brindle-colored backside.

"Okay, pretty girl," he cooed at her "Let's make some potties and then go get mommy. Grey has a plan, and a cheeseburger in the car just waiting on you. I know, I know. Mommy's going to be pissed when she finds out I gave you a cheeseburger, but whose fault is that? Hers. That's who. She should have stayed home where she belonged. Right, little lady?"

As he strode down the dark stairwell and out the door, remembering Morsey's words about the girl gang of women got him thinking…

~

"So?" Nina prodded with a leer. "Any explanations for how the guy who wanted to take you out knows your friend and you?"

What was going on? She could think of no one—*no one*—who wanted to kill her. But apparently, somebody wanted to kill her.

And what did those words mean? *Samantha told me*

you were a nosy bitch… Was it someone who was connected with Samantha's disappearance? How had they found out about her?

Sal was stunned into silence, but Nina wasn't going to let go. Instead, she plopped down next to Sal and leaned into her to let her know who was the boss of this interrogation.

"Waiting."

"Processing," Sal replied with a tremble in her voice she hated.

"Thinking about your death?" Nina responded with a glare.

Sal winced. "Hoping you'll reconsider."

"Give me one fucking good reason."

But she had no explanation. None, and the idea someone had said those words about her left her afraid and very clear about how alone she truly was. Taking a ragged breath, she looked Nina directly in the eye with a plea in hers.

"Listen, I'm telling you, I don't know who'd want to harm me. I swear, I only wanted to find out about the baby and his well-being. I don't even know what happened to Samantha or how she died. After I made sure the baby was all right, that was the next thing I planned to look into. But on my life, I don't know what's going on."

Nina sniffed around Sal again. "But you're afraid."

"Yes. I'm afraid," she admitted. Why deny what Nina already knew? "Look, it's just me now since Samantha's gone. I don't have anyone else but my dog. If someone's trying to hurt me because of Samantha, that makes no sense at all because she never introduced me to anyone new, but I won't lie and say it doesn't scare me."

Nina sat back on the couch and crossed her legs. "So all those seedy people you mentioned from your bar, you think one of them might know more than they're lettin' on about what happened to Samantha? Because if the dude knew to look here for you, and you're connected to Samantha, it has to have some shit to do with the baby. Which means you brought your bad mojo here and put the baby in danger. For that, you gotta die," she hissed, reaching for Sal's throat.

"Nina! Nooo!" Marty yelled, just as she dove for the couch and grabbed Nina's wrist, yanking her backward to keep her from strangling Sal, who jumped to her feet and rolled over the arm of the sofa, knocking the lamp down.

"Get off me, Blondie, or I'm gonna rip those fake eyelashes off your big flirty eyes!"

In the midst of the chaos, as Nina and Marty struggled, the doorbell rang, making everyone freeze on the spot.

Marty blew her hair from her face and huffed a ragged breath, still holding on to Nina's wrist.

Nina yanked her wrist away from Marty's grasp as Heath went to answer the door, shaking his head.

Wanda stood in front of Sal—who'd rolled to the floor and then to her feet—to protect her, and sent daggers of death at Nina with her eyes.

As Heath opened the door, Sal almost passed out.

"Good evening, sir. I'm Officer Muncey. Sorry to disturb you so late. We're talking to everyone in the neighborhood tonight about a disturbance someone witnessed about a half hour ago. May I come in and ask you some questions?"

Sal froze. He might have changed his appearance, but he'd kept his voice—a gravelly voice that had whispered in her ear many a time.

She was going to kill him. Eviscerate him. No, wait. Maybe she'd invite Nina to do it for her. Maybe she'd eat his face off. His face had to be more filling than hers. He, after all, had two of them.

Heath motioned him inside, his expression a mask of unreadable emotions. "Of course, Officer. How can we help?"

Grey, disguised as a police officer who'd eaten too many donuts, with Buttercup in tow, stepped inside the entryway to the Jeffersons'. Buttercup made eye contact with Sal, but Grey kept a tight rein on her leash to keep her from greeting her mistress.

"You don't mind animals, do you, sir? I assure you, Buttercup's very friendly unless ordered otherwise," Grey asked, his eyes meeting hers with a twinkle of devilish glee in them.

"We love 'em," Nina assured with a happy grin, holding the back of her hand out for Buttercup to sniff.

And as per usual Buttercup MO, she rubbed her wide head against Nina's thigh in happy grunts, accepting any and all forms of affection.

"Who is this beautiful baby? Are you a good police

doggie, Precious? Can you smell the bad guys? Maybe you should sniff around and see if we have any here, huh?" Nina chirped in a high-pitched tone, rubbing Buttercup's ears while giving Sal an angry glare.

Sal's heart throbbed in her chest, throbbed so hard she was sure everyone could hear it, even as Heath answered all of Grey's questions.

When he finished with Heath, who'd for some unknown reason covered for her, he turned to Sal, putting her on the spot.

"Do you live here, too, Miss...?" He stopped, waiting for her to fill in the blanks as though this were some game he was rather enjoying.

Her cheeks went red and hot. "Brice. Sally Brice, and no. I don't live here. I'm just..." She paused and looked at everyone around her, waiting for them to accuse her of impersonating a social worker, but everyone remained strangely silent. "Visiting," she provided. "I'm just visiting."

He cocked a bushy eyebrow at her, lifting his rounded chin. "As I told Mr. Jefferson, I'm afraid you match the description we were given by a witness. He told me you could explain. May I speak with you outside for a moment, please, Miss Brice?"

She bit the inside of her cheek to keep from calling him Grey, among other names. "Sure, *Officer Muncey*. I'd be delighted to join you outside with—Buttercup, is it?" She smiled down at her dog, all the while sending a signal there'd be no Snausages for her tonight.

As she followed him out the door, Wanda called out, "Would you like me to go with you?"

Grey turned and tipped his official police officer hat at Wanda with an amicable smile and a nod. "I'd prefer you let me speak to Miss Brice alone. I promise to get her right back to you as soon as this is all cleared up—which I'm sure it will be."

Letting him lead the way, Grey walked to the end of the cheerfully lit pathway and behind a large boxwood hedge at the end of the driveway before he turned to look at her.

And then he growled as he morphed back into his own body, "You get your sweet butt in my car now before you damn well blow this sky high, Sal! Jesus, you know I can only skin-surf for a few minutes at a time! Do you really want to see me go down in flames?" He pointed a finger to his car parked just a couple of yards down the road and out of sight of the house.

Buttercup whined at him. She hated discord and upset almost as much as Sal did, but she soothed her by stroking her ear and made a face at Grey. "Nice badge, *Officer*."

"I said get in the car!" He whisper-yelled the demand.

"Or what?" She was feeling pretty ballsy after telling the Jeffersons the truth. What did she have to lose?

"Or," he hissed, snatching her by the waist to haul her up over his shoulder fireman's style, "I'll take you there myself! Dammit, Sal, do you have any idea the shit you're in the middle of?"

As she bounced off his hard back, and Buttercup trotted happily beside them, she gripped the edge of his shirt and yelled at his delicious backside, "Put me down, you jerk!"

He did just that, unceremoniously dropping her right onto the hood of his car, his nostrils flaring as his eyes glittered under the moonlight. He bracketed her hips with his hands as he leaned in close and menacing. "I promise you, Sal, I'll tie your ass up if I have to in order to keep you away from these people. Do you hear me? I'll damn well do it."

Instead of reacting out of anger, she looked up at him and smiled. "I didn't out you, if that's what you're so worried about. But I did tell them the truth about who I am."

His eyes flashed dark and hot at her. "I'm going to strangle you, Sal Brice. What will it take to get it through your thick skull, you're messing with dangerous people here?"

His words surprised her. "You mean the Jeffersons? How can they be considered dangerous? Unless you mean Nina, well, yeah. She's certainly dangerous, but I don't think she'd really *hurt me,* hurt me. Do you?"

His jaw tightened and began to tic. "Yes. No. I don't know. The point is, you promised to go home."

She gave him an offended look. "I was going home until someone hit me on the head. That madwoman Nina rescued me from whoever it was that tried to knock my skull in. Or so she says, anyway. They had me cornered in there, Grey, at their total mercy. What was I supposed to do? I had no choice but to give it up. Nina can smell when you're not telling the truth. Or something of that nature. She's a vampire and she scares the shit out of me. Whatever. The point is, I didn't give *you* up."

His sigh was ragged and drawn out. "That's not the point anymore, Sal. Who do you suppose would want to hurt you? I did tell you I deal with some very dangerous informants, didn't I?"

Now her eyes narrowed in suspicion. "But how would they know who I am?"

"Some of my informants are bad guys, Brice. What if you led them right to the Jeffersons and the baby? You don't think some dirty informants wouldn't mind kidnapping a rare zombie baby for ransom, do you?"

Her heart began to thrum erratically. If she'd put the baby's life in danger, she'd never be able to live with herself.

But hold on, Nina said the man had said, "Samantha told me you were a nosy bitch."

And why the hell would Grey be concerned about the guy connecting her to the Jeffersons if he didn't already know something about the guy who'd almost bashed her head in?

Something was so wrong about this—so wrong. Grey was trying too hard to keep her from the Jeffersons under the guise of protecting his own hide from the council.

And upon reflection, he had said she didn't know the shit she was in the middle of, hadn't he? He'd also said they—whoever "they" were—were dangerous people.

Leaning back, she rested on her palms, the heat from the engine of his car soaking into her skin, and looked up at him. "So here's a question, Grey. What aren't you telling me?"

CHAPTER 6

"Forget it, Hamlin. Cover fucking blown," a voice from just beyond Grey's shoulder said.

Grey drove the heel of his hand against his rusty car and stood upright, making her jump.

As the man who belonged to the voice appeared out of the shadows, tall and hulking, Sal didn't know whether to run in fear or find out what cover had been blown.

"Dammit, Sal," Grey muttered before turning to the large man. "Did McCall call it off?"

"You bet your ass he did, and he wants this one and that bunch in there in protective custody. We can't take a chance they'll end up hurt."

"What the hell is going on, Grey?" she blurted out. "And who is this?"

The man smiled at her, his chestnut-brown hair slicked back from his angular face. "Agent Carr

Morsey, ma'am. Pleasure. Sorry for the crude language."

She looked at both men, utterly astounded, and blinked.

"Close your mouth, Sal. It's mosquito season," Grey remarked before pulling his phone from his pocket.

Slipping from the hood of the car, she watched and listened as the two of them discussed something about this McCall person and protective custody so casually, she thought she'd explode.

When a lull in the conversation occurred, she gripped Grey's arm and forced him to look at her. "Again, I ask, *what the hell's going on, Grey?*"

"Wanna know what's going on, Sal? Here's what's going on. I'm an idiot. Straight up, I take full responsibility for what's gone down. I should never have told you anything about Samantha's baby, not even a little—no matter how doe-eyed and sad panda you were. I should have known you'd snoop around when I wasn't looking and find that file. But I did. And I'm taking responsibility for that, because now it's going to be my job to keep you and those people safe from these lunatics because I couldn't resist you."

Buttercup rubbed up against her thigh in a possessive gesture, forcing her to stay focused—because her brain was on overdrive. He couldn't resist her? Well, that was some newsflash. He'd broken up with her. She couldn't be *that* irresistible.

But wait. Hadn't he said it was his job to keep her

safe from the lunatics? "You're job? How is it a private detective's job to keep me safe?"

Closing his eyes, Grey planted his hands on his lean hips then opened them again as if it took the patience of Job to explain to her. "I'm not a private detective. I'm an agent with a paranormal task force doing undercover work—which I let you totally muck up by giving you information I shouldn't have. That's how it's my job to keep you safe."

Task force?

An agent?

Like James Bond kind of agent?

What in all of fresh hell was going on?

~

"Sit, please," Wanda insisted, waving her hand at the rustic farmhouse table that had to be at least ten feet long.

Carr and Grey had gathered everyone inside in order to explain to them what Sal still couldn't wrap her head around.

Ever gracious, The Jeffersons insisted they sit and talk with everyone, treating them in the same manner they'd treated her. With respect and kindness.

Archibald had made tea and brought a plate filled with assorted cookies, his weary eyes bloodshot from lack of sleep. "Please, gentleman, you must be hungry. Eat. I'm sure being on stakeout works up an appetite."

Stakeout. They'd been watching her every move.

She felt like she was in some cop movie every time Grey and Carr used words like surveillance and perpetrator.

Sal sat between Nina and Grey, still in shock. The gist of this was, Grey was an undercover agent for some secret paranormal task force, investigating paranormal trafficking, as was his hot partner Carr, a werewolf, if anyone cared to know.

"Okay," Nina said as she rocked the baby, who'd had a bottle with the brains Sal had provided and seemed thoroughly content now as he slept against her breast. His dark head, with hair so like Samantha's, made her heart hurt. "So what you're telling us is, you investigate paranormal trafficking? Particularly, the trafficking of paranormal women. Like, seriously? Who the eff would try to traffic a paranormal, dude? We're not exactly weaklings."

"Usually another paranormal," Grey responded, taking a bite of a shortbread cookie. "There are plenty of dark paranormals out there, Nina. Plenty of people willing to make a buck off their own kind. It's not that much different than human trafficking, if you think about it."

Heath took the baby when Nina handed him off, placing him against his chest and rubbing his cheek against the soft down of his head as he listened. "And you're investigating this how? What does it all have to do with Sal and us?"

Carr rested his elbows on the table and folded his hands together, his face solemn, his green-blue eyes almost angry. "This has been a long time coming, Mr. Jefferson. We've worked for months on this case just to get a decent lead. It just so happened Sal, who works in a questionable establishment, began asking around after her friend Samantha disappeared. We have informants all over the place, and when she tipped one of them off, and Samantha's disappearance had all the characteristics we look for in trafficking, we made sure Sal came to us so we could investigate her."

Ooooo, Monty! It had to have been that rat bastard Monty. He'd been more than happy to give her Grey's name as she handed him a hundred-dollar bill.

"Monty's an informant?" Sal squeaked.

Not a day went by that Monty wasn't sidled up to her bar, whiskey neat in his hand, yakking her ear off. Go figure. Though, if it meant he'd helped in some way with finding who'd taken Samantha, she was grateful.

Grey dipped his dark head as he sipped at his tea, the warmth of it making his olive skin go ruddy around his cheeks. "That's exactly what Monty is. So when you began asking around about where to go to get help to find Samantha, he sent you to me."

"And that was planned. I sort of walked right into this, right?" Sal asked, barely able to look at Grey just yet. This was all too new, too raw.

Carr confirmed by nodding his head. "Yes. We fed the informant information about a detective who could possibly help you, he gave it to you, and that led you to Agent Hamlin."

Agent Hamlin. She'd slept with some weird paranormal version of the FBI. She guessed sleeping with someone, even an unwitting participant in the investigation, was a no-no.

Rubbing her hands over her eyes, she resisted yawning from exhaustion. "And I gave him as much information as I possibly could about Samantha, which only helped you two."

"That's right. Hearing how Samantha behaved before she disappeared, her anger with you when you tried to pry into her odd comings and goings, the rapid change in her usually open personality, is always cause to wonder if she'd been in the process of a grooming. That she's a rare hybrid zombie made us even more suspicious."

"Grooming?" Marty chirped, sitting up straight in her chair.

Nina reached out and grabbed Sal's hand, taking her by surprise. "Yeah. Like wooing or courting her. Saying all the right things. Trying to get her to hook up with him and such. He was prepping her for the time when he'd..." She squeezed Sal's hand and didn't let go.

Licking her lips, her mouth as dry as any desert, Sal began to get the picture. "You mean like those animals do online with childr... Oh, God. Oh, God, no. No, no, no..." she murmured, unable to catch her breath. The realization, the sheer horror hit her square in the gut, tearing at her insides.

Trafficking. As in, they'd snatched Samantha up and they'd let people do deplorable things to her for money. Oh, God.

She fell forward, holding her stomach to keep from retching.

Nina pulled Sal's chair closer to hers and wrapped an arm around her shoulder. "Breathe, Social Worker. We'll figure this out. We'll find who did this and obliterate them."

But the vampire's assurances weren't enough. Nothing would ever be enough. Nothing but finding the son of a bitch and castrating him. Hurting him. Making him scream in agony just like Samantha had in her vision just before she'd died.

Grey reached out a hand to cup her shoulder, too, and she was too weak to pull away even if she wanted to. "I'm sorry, Sal. I didn't do this to hurt you. I didn't lie to you because I wanted to. I *had* to. You were our only in, and as we went over Samantha's online chats and phone texts, we knew we were on to something."

Sal's head popped up. "You have a record of her online chats? How can that be? I went through everything she had. Every square inch of her belongings and her computer. Everything, and I found nothing."

Grey's lips thinned in obvious disgust. "You were meant to find nothing. We made sure of it to keep you safe. Look, that you're even here is partially my fault, and I apologize to all concerned for putting you in danger. I won't rest until I'm sure you're all safe."

"So you're who told Sal where the baby was? How did you figure that out? The adoption agency makes it sound like their records are kept at Fort Knox," Wanda said, leaning into Heath to rub the baby's tiny back.

"Don't blame him for what I did. Please," Sal defended, her eyes grainy from lack of sleep. "I was so torn up by the phone call she made to me, asking me to save the baby, and then with the vision of her death, I turned into a total wreck. Meltdown status is more like it. He only told me about you and Heath, and he was vague, because he knew it would ease my mind that if nothing else, the baby was safe. But I took it a step further and sort of dug around his files and got the information when he wasn't around. I promised myself I wouldn't come looking, but...and now... I didn't know. I swear, I didn't know any of this."

Wanda reached a hand across the table, her kind eyes connecting with Sal's. "It's okay. Please, honey, don't apologize again. I won't hear it."

Carr wiped his mouth with a napkin, crinkling it in his lean, tanned fingers. "It wasn't long after Sal had the vision that we got a tip about an abandoned baby at some rest area off the Jersey turnpike. An unusual baby —one who would, and forgive my frankness, sell for millions. From there, we just followed the trail to the adoption agency, and of course we recognized the baby because of his birthmark. It was almost as if whoever left the baby wanted us to find him, and we just didn't get there in time."

Grey ran a hand through his hair, his eyes softer but his jaw tight when he looked to her. "I didn't tell you any of this because I knew it would only put you in danger, Sal. We...*I* couldn't afford to have you go in guns blazing. But I knew how torn up you were about Samantha. I couldn't stand watching you suffer."

"Cover the little dude's ears, Wanda," Nina instructed, then turned to Grey. "So some mother-fucking animal courted this Samantha, kidnapped her, and forced her to have a kid? Is that what you're fucking telling us?"

Grey didn't hesitate with his answer. "Essentially, yes."

"And the dude who whacked her tonight? Who the fuck is he, and how does he relate to this shit? He's human, you know. I smelled the asshole just before he took off, and I would have beat his weak ass if I wasn't so worried she was gonna end up brain dead."

"We think it's the birth father," Grey said point-blank. "We're pretty sure he somehow lost the baby he was supposed to give to the traffickers, and the description Carr gave me fits the guy who was hanging around Samantha just before she disappeared. We think he's always known who Sal was, and he followed her to you."

The guilt of what she'd done would never leave her. She'd never let a day pass when she didn't beat herself up for doing exactly what she'd promised Grey she wouldn't do.

But about this guy… "The guy she was hanging around? There was never a guy!" Sal protested, her stomach rolling with anxiety, her throat closing with acrid bile. "She would have told me about a guy!"

"There was a guy, Sal," Carr assured her. "The same

guy she was chatting with online was seen with her near a bar in Brooklyn. I know it's hard to hear your best friend didn't share everything with you, but in this case, it's the truth."

Her entire world rocked at that point. Samantha's last days, maybe even as long as a month, had been bizarre, and at the time, she'd been more hurt than suspicious anything nefarious was going down.

To hear Samantha had met someone—that she'd trusted someone, talked to them, maybe even developed feelings for them, hurt. It hurt something fierce that her friend hadn't shared that with her.

"So, she went off with this guy and he got her pregnant and then what?" Sal managed to ask as her whole body shook with rage.

"She had the baby, and we suspect the father was either going to sell him to the highest trafficking bidder, or he's in deep with the traffickers and he was supposed to show up with a baby. Then Samantha called you—and we still don't know how she got her hands on a phone—then she died. But someone got to the baby before that maggot could and dropped him off at a rest area. We have no leads on who got their hands on him and got him to safety," Carr said.

Nina tightened her hold on Sal's shoulders, her cool skin brushing against her cheek. "So he was going to sell his own damn flesh and blood? For some fucking cash?"

Grey's expression went grim, his eyes dark. "That's the best explanation we have. Usually, the groomer solely handles his victim. So likely, he kept her locked away somewhere until she had the baby. If I know anything about these traffickers, I know they'll kill him if he doesn't produce. I'd say he's desperate. The one thing we know for sure? He's a loose cannon. We're hoping because he's so volatile, he'll do something stupid again like he did tonight."

Sal frowned, her hand trembling. "So you've both been watching me? You saw him attack me tonight?"

"I did, but just the tail end of it," Carr confirmed, then hitched his jaw at Nina. "Thankfully, this lady was there to help you. I went after him, but he slipped through my fingers and I lost him."

"Which means he's going to come back and maybe try to take my baby," Wanda whispered, but then her face went hard and her eyes fierce with hatred as she stroked the baby's head. "I'll kill him, you know. I'll mutilate him."

Nina popped her lips as her nostrils flared. "Nobody's taking anybody anywhere, Wanda. Because I'll kill the fuck before he takes his next breath."

Marty reached out for her friend, tugging her into her grip, her eyes watery. "No one, I do mean no one, will hurt a hair on his head. I promise you."

But Grey held up a hand. "These people are dangerous, Mrs. Jefferson. It's not just the father you need to worry about. He's human, and surely you could take care of him if the need arises. But there are others involved. Others like yourselves, and they won't hesitate to kill you to keep themselves hidden from council."

"Please," Nina scoffed in clear disgust, cracking her knuckles. "Like I haven't dealt with scum like them before? You should see what the fuck I've seen. And I'm still standin', boys. I'm not afraid of these panty wastes."

Carr's chair scraped on the hardwood floor as he pushed it back and rose. "I don't doubt that, Mrs. Statleon. Not for a second. However, council has asked us to keep watch on their esteemed members, meaning all of you. You're valuable to our community and highly regarded. We need you safe so you can continue the work you do. Most importantly, we need the baby safe."

"So what does that mean for us?" Heath asked, rising as well, his expression grim.

Grey answered, his tone somber. "It means no one leaves here without one of us until further notice, Mr. Jefferson."

But Sal wasn't hearing much of anything at this point. Samantha had been trafficked. Some sick bastard had used and abused her and made her carry a child like some kind of brood mare.

The very thought of gentle Samantha—sweet, kind, easygoing Samantha—forced to...

Sal didn't think she could bear the visual those words summoned. She wanted to crawl out of her skin, scream, cry, run and hide under the covers of her bed.

And then she wanted the vile pig to die just like

Samantha had. She wanted to hear his screams, bash his head in and dance in his brains.

That's what she wanted with every breath left in her.

She wanted him to suffer agonies he'd never suffered before—and she wanted to be the one to spit in his face just before she killed him.

CHAPTER 7

Nina nudged her shoulder as she sat in the now quiet living room in the semi-dark. She'd been slumped on the couch with Buttercup curled up beside her since they'd ended their conversation and Grey and Carr had set up shop in the Jeffersons' dining room.

"Shitty question, but are you all right, dude?"

"I don't know if I'll ever be all right again." How could she be all right knowing Samantha had suffered, quite possibly for months? How?

"You will. *You will.* I know you don't see that now, but you will," she urged in her husky voice.

"I don't know if I want to," she said, her misery so rife, so raw, she almost couldn't move. "I can't get the vision of her out of my head. I can't stop creating visuals of all the horrible things..."

Nina gripped her hand and squeezed. "Yep. I get it. But you have to, Sal. The baby needs to know your friend, where he came from, and you're his best bet for that. Don't make him suffer because of this. And I promise you, one day you'll replace all the shitty stuff with all the good shit you've got stored up there in your head."

"How could I have missed this?" she whispered into the dimly lit room on a ragged breath. "How could I have not known this thing with Samantha was about a man?"

"People do crazy shit, Sal, especially when it involves a damn man. She didn't want you to know. That's how you didn't know."

Covering her face with her hands, she didn't even bother to stop the tears she shed. "But why? *Why?* We never hid anything from each other." Never.

Nina snorted as though she had the answer. "You know what my experience is with shit like that? She was ashamed. She knew you wouldn't approve—maybe you'd tell her the guy was no good for her, and who wants to hear that gripe when you're all up to your elbows and unicorns in love? She'd call you jealous because you didn't have a dude of your own. It's the same old shit that always happens when a chick finds a guy her friends know is wrong for her. And likely, this motherfucking dick was busy isolating her, telling her you wouldn't approve because you were jealous—or afraid she'd leave you. It's what weak fucks like that do."

In hindsight, that made perfect sense. Samantha was so hungry for love, so hungry for a home and family of her own, it made sense whoever this douche was would play on those desperate desires and eat them like they were a snack.

"She was such a good person. She was so sweet, so trusting…I…"

Nina patted her thigh. "I bet she was. I hope you'll tell me all about her someday. Especially because she's like my Carl."

Carl. She'd forgotten about him, but he was a loose connection to Samantha's heritage, and she really wanted to meet him. "He's supposed to be here tomorrow, right?"

"Yep. You'll like him. He'll like you, and he can't wait to meet the baby. My Carl loves to read. The baby will never want for a bedtime story."

That made Sal smile.

"So tell me about you and Agent Fifty Shades," Nina demanded bluntly.

She'd laugh at the vampire's play on words for the popular book, but her heart turned over again, only this time, there was only turmoil and that incessant ache she'd had since they'd broken up.

"There's not much to tell. Obviously, he used me to get information about Samantha. And I don't blame him for that. His cause is good."

"Right, but were you two ridin' the roller coaster while he was doing all this investigating undercover?"

"Do you mean were we sleeping together?"

"Call it whatever you like. I'm trying to use sensitive

fucking words because that's what I hear people like. So yeah, did ya do him?"

Oh, had she ever—over and over—much to her chagrin, now that she knew who he really was. "Yes," she replied, then her cheeks went hot. "We did have a relationship of sorts."

"And now you don't."

Fighting the shudder of her inhale, Sal shook her head. "Now we don't."

"He's still hot for you. Just so you know."

"Really? Does someone who's hot for you break up with you?"

"They do if they're lookin' out for your ass. It's clear he was watchin' out for you. That's what a good guy does, Sal. Like it or leave it, but that's his truth."

God, she wanted to believe. But she couldn't. "I don't think that's the case, but if you think he's hot for me, I believe you."

"You're still hot for him, too."

"I'm still too raw to even consider how I feel about him."

"Bullshit, but you do whatever it takes to protect yourself from being hurt again."

When Sal could only nod numbly, because addressing Grey and her feelings was too much after tonight's revelation, Nina asked another question. "Mind if I ask you a question about Samantha?"

A change of subject was okay by her. "Of course."

"Did she lose body parts everywhere? How the hell did she keep from being discovered by humans? Swear to Christ, every time I turn around, my kid's losing a digit in front of someone—usually a human someone. It's damned hard to keep that shit hidden, and we have no idea why his body parts just fall the fuck off. He's such a mystery."

Sal smiled sadly. "You mean discovered by her skin color, right? Samantha used to tell humans she had a skin condition. As we got older, she covered it with makeup and turtlenecks, even in the summer, and yeah, once she lost her thumb in the toilet at a Knicks game. It was hysterical," she recalled on a laugh. "We spent most of the game trying to find Scotch tape or glue because she left her purse at home with what we jokingly called her 'first-aid kit' still inside. I don't think we've ever laughed as hard as we did that night."

"Carl's index and pinky finger fell off in the middle of Macy's, straight in front of this old lady. Swear, I thought she'd shit an entire white sale right there in front of us," Nina admitted on a cackle.

Sal laughed at that, too, and then she sobered. It almost felt wrong to laugh now that Samantha was dead.

Then Nina nudged her again. "Told ya you'd remember good things. Now, you get some sleep. Wait. Do banshees sleep? I know shit-all about you lot."

"There's not a lot to know other than death visits us far more than we'd like. We don't have super-strength or fangs or heightened senses of smell. But we do sleep. Unlike vampires, we need our Zzz's."

"Then I'll sit with you until you fall asleep."

Somehow, as frightened as she had been by Nina, now that thought comforted her. "Will you?" she was almost afraid to ask. No one had ever offered to console her before, and the feeling was warm and scary all at once.

"I will."

"You really are a marshmallow like Marty accused, aren't you?" Sal asked as she leaned her head back on the sofa and hunkered down on the soft cushions.

Nina dragged a hand-knit blanket over her and tucked it under her chin. "Spent some time in therapy last year after I lost my vampirism. Gained twenty damn pounds and got a pain-in-the-ass familiar to show for it—but I learned shit along the way."

Ah. Right. She remembered now. Nina was also half witch.

But then she processed her words. "*You* were in therapy? You?" Sal was shocked to hear this volatile woman would even consider professional help.

"Yep, and I'm not even gonna wring your neck about that tone in your voice—because violence is never acceptable. Well, until it is."

Sal wiped a residual tear from her cheek, curious about this strange yet sympathetic woman. "And you lost your vampirism, but you got it back?"

"That happened, too. I've come a long way this last year."

She swallowed and burrowed down into the couch. "Did therapy help you, Nina?"

"Yeah. It did. I've learned to accept some shit—the

marshmallow crap is just part of that. And as much as I don't like that part of it, there it is. But don't let it get around. Because I'll have to kill you if you go spreadin' fuckin' lies."

Sal chuckled again and closed her eyes, stroking Buttercup's velvety-soft ears and leaning into Nina. "Thank you, Nina."

"Not a thing, kiddo. Not a thing," she replied, reaching once more for Sal's hand and tucking it into her cool palm until Sal's pulse slowed and she relaxed into sleep.

~

Upon waking the next day, a gray mist still in the early morning air, dew still on the grass, Sal sat for a moment and let the silence of the house surround her.

Nina was gone, but her presence last night had meant everything—*everything*. No one but Samantha had ever been there for her—comforted her—in quite that way until last night. That warmth lingered even now, hugging her tight, and she wasn't quite ready to let it go.

Buttercup sighed next to her, her muscled body relaxed in sleep, but she'd be up soon needing a morning walk and the spell would be broken. Slipping from the couch, she ordered her to stay as she went to find a bathroom and at least splash some cold water on her face, if not use some toothpaste and her finger to brush her teeth.

As she went through the dining room where all the computers and such were set up, but Grey and Carr were nowhere in sight, and into the incredible kitchen, she paused. The kitchen was spectacular, with more antiqued white cabinets and miles of soapstone countertops adorned with light blue veins running through them than she'd ever seen in her life. Wanda and Heath busied themselves at the kitchen sink as Archibald whipped up something on the six-burner stove.

That was when Sal caught sight of a bassinette by the French doors, and a tiny fist flying in the air.

Softly, she padded toward the tiny blue crib and peeked inside, getting her first real full glimpse of Samantha's beautiful baby, and instantly choked up.

He'd been so discontent yesterday, he'd spent most of it with his face buried in one shoulder or another, and she'd only caught quick glimpses of him. But today —today he was wreathed in smiles and sweet coos. The slight green tint to his skin was paired with the rosy pink of his cheeks. His dark hair, so much the color of Samantha's, sprouted from his head in thick thatches, soft and silky.

"Ohhhh, look at you. You're perfect," she breathed, clinging to his small fist when he batted it at her, her gut grew tight with emotion and her heart filled with instant love. "Oh, little one, you have no idea how much your mother would love you, how perfect she'd think you are. How perfect I think you are."

He grunted and stretched, flashing his gummy grin at her, turning her heart inside out in her chest.

Tucking her hair behind her ear, Sal pulled a chair closer to the bassinette and leaned over to rub his soft fist against her cheek and inhale his sweet baby scent. "I promise to tell you everything one day. Everything you want to know about her. All the things she loved. All the things she'd want you to know growing up as a zombie. I swear I'd take you if I could, but...you deserve so much more than I have. I have a crappy apartment in Brooklyn and I work as a bartender. Definitely not the kind of job a respectable mom has. Last I checked, there was a bottle of ketchup and a moldy container of cottage cheese in my fridge. I'd rather eat a juicy bacon cheeseburger than quinoa and organic chicken. I sleep on a pullout sofa, and I forget to do my laundry until I'm down to one pair of underwear and then it's all-out panic. I don't have a savings account or even more than one hundred and fifty dollars in my checking account at any given time. All this to say, I'd be an awful bet, buddy."

He cooed at her, kicking his chubby legs in response.

Closing her eyes, Sal inhaled. "But these people—the Jeffersons—they'll love you so, so much. You'll have tons of people to help take care of you and a beautiful house to live and grow up in, in a neighborhood that looks like it's straight up *Brady Bunch*. They'll teach you what it is to be good and honorable—honest. Just like your mom. And you'll have cousins and family dinners, and big Christmases and…and so many wonderful things—all the things your mother would have wanted for you. But I hope…no, I pray…someday, you'll want to know me, too. Because I love you. Just as much as I loved your mother. We were all each other had for a long, long time. Maybe someday, I…" She drew a breath, fighting a sob. "Well, maybe someday, I can take you for ice cream—your mother loved ice cream. I'm betting you will, too."

A warm hand settled on her back, before Wanda said, "I hope you'll see him before he can eat ice cream. We haven't even gotten past brains yet. I feel like ice cream's at least a few months away," she said on a soft laugh.

Sal laughed too, swiping at her eyes as Wanda settled in a chair near hers. "I don't want to interfere, Mrs. Jefferson—"

Looking as beautiful as if she'd had a full night's rest, Wanda shook her finger at Sal. "First, it's Wanda. Mrs. Jefferson makes me sound ancient. Which I will be one day, but that day is not today. Second, I meant what I said. There's no secrecy here. The baby will always know where he came from and that he was loved before adoption and after. He'll know there were circumstances beyond Samantha's control—beyond your control—that kept him from being with either of you. By extension, you're an aunt, and you can never really have enough of those to spoil you, can you?"

Her heart twisted in her chest. They hardly knew her, and yet, they were allowing her access to her last link to Samantha with such graciousness and compassion, she almost couldn't bear it—especially after she'd duped them.

"I don't think you'll ever know how much that means to me, Mrs. Je—er, Wanda."

On impulse, she hugged her, clenching her eyes tight to prevent more gushing tears as she inhaled Wanda's light floral perfume. She'd cried more in these last months than she ever had in her entire life.

Rising, Wanda scooped up the baby and set him in Sal's arms after a quick cuddle. "I meant what I said last night. Those weren't just words, Sal. He's as important to you as he is to us, and we can't, as thinking, breathing beings, ever have enough love."

"Can I ask a personal question?"

"Of course."

"Why adoption? Aren't you half werewolf? Marty has a little girl..."

Wanda tilted her head and smiled. "Before I was accidentally turned, and I say that loosely, I had ovarian cancer. Since then, I've not been able to conceive. There's no medical explanation for why I can't. It just hasn't happened, and the speculation that my cancer prior to turning is a factor made us decide to look into other alternatives. I had a hole in my heart, Sal, one needing filling. Now, with the baby, it's filled so full. Even with all the upset and my crazy fears from yesterday."

"What about surrogacy?"

"Oh, we talked about that—Marty even offered, as

did my sister, and I'm not opposed at all. But here's the thing, when I began to research and found out how many children, not just human, but paranormal, needed homes, it felt right—it fit. And we don't plan to stop at just one. We have a lot of love to give, Sal Brice."

"You're an amazing lady, Wanda," Sal said in awe.

But Wanda shook her head and dismissed the notion with a grin. "I'm nothing of the sort. Now," she said, leaning down to press a kiss on the baby's head. "You stay here with Auntie Sal, and Mommy's going to go see if we've identified the person who needs a new asshole chewed. Be a good boy."

With that, Wanda went off to handle whatever assholes she meant to handle in a swirl of pretty sundress and pearls, leaving Sal to hold a baby.

A baby. She'd never held a baby.

"Mistress Sal, support under the head at all times," Archibald said as he placed her hand under the baby's tiny skull and beamed down at her. He looked tired, but immaculate as ever. "That's it. Look at you. You're an absolute natural. Now, might I interest you in fluffy scrambled eggs as light and airy as clouds on a warm summer day, and a freshly made hickory and hazelnut coffee? My own special brew, of course. Perhaps toast and homemade apricot jam as well?"

Sal smiled as the baby snuggled against her breast and her heart exploded. "That would be awesome, but first, is there somewhere I can freshen up? I'd just like to splash some water on my face, maybe use some mouthwash?"

Archibald smoothed his hands over the lapels of his crisp black jacket and laughed. "In this house, where Bobbie-Sue and Pack Cosmetics own at least a hundred shares in the downstairs powder room alone? I should say we do. I've prepared toiletries, a toothbrush, fresh towels, and a change of clothes. You look almost the same size and stature as our fair Marty. She leaves clothes here for her overnights and surely won't mind loaning them out. Now hand me that rapscallion and off with you. Breakfast awaits!"

She handed the squirming baby to Archibald and thanked him, making her way to the bathroom off the kitchen. Closing the door, she leaned back on it and inhaled before giving herself a critical once over in the mirror at her smudged mascara and smeared lipstick.

Digging in her pocket, she pulled out a hairband and dragged her hair into a ponytail before turning on the water.

Archibald was right, there were Bobbie-Sue lotions and moisturizers everywhere, including some from Pack Cosmetics, too, on a small tray atop the vanity, making her wonder if the shares crack had some connection.

One long, hard look at herself after she'd scrubbed her face and changed into Marty's jeans and flowing sweater, and she was almost sure she was ready to face the day.

Except...someone had tried to hurt her last night. Hurt was probably the wrong term. He'd probably aimed to kill her. She was just one more person in the way of him getting his hands on the baby.

Sitting on the top of the top of the toilet seat she gripped the cool porcelain of the vanity and let her head fall between her shoulders.

Someone had tried to kill her.

Last night's bravado had turned to today's fear. How would she protect herself from someone who wanted to kill her? She didn't have the abilities the others had, like super-strength.

As she pondered this, her body suddenly stiffened, making her grip the vanity harder, until her knuckles were white and her hands shook.

No. Not now. Not today. Please not today.

And then her mouth opened wide, and she screamed as wave after wave of vibration struck every nerve in her body.

Screamed until the glass bottles around her shook and the mirror broke in splintering shards of flying glass.

Her eyes rolled to the back of her head and her teeth chattered as she was sucked into a vision. A dismal, dark vision she literally experienced as though she were in the very room in which it was taking place.

And her last thought before she slid to the tiled floor was, *Oh, God, please no.*

CHAPTER 8

"Sal! Open the door! Sal!" Grey yelled, until he gave up waiting for an answer and used his shoulder to break the door open, only to find her slumped on the tile, her head at an awkward angle.

He dragged her upward and sat on the toilet seat, pulling her into his arms, pressing her head against his shoulder. Lifting her wrist, he felt for a pulse and found one, steady as a rock. Breathing a sigh of relief, he kept her close, reluctant to let her go.

"Jesus and a can of Spam, what the fuck was that?" Nina crowed from outside the door as everyone gathered to see what had happened.

Grey held her close, inhaling her scent, waiting for her to wake up. "I think that was the death scream she once told me about. They're hard on her."

Nina stuck a finger in her ear and said, "Fuck, I think my eardrums exploded. Is she okay?"

Hoisting her up off the floor, he nodded. "I think she'll be okay, though the last vision she had, the one of Samantha dying, left her blacked out for two days, according to her."

Marty gasped and pushed to door wide open, her eyes full of concern. "Bring her out to the couch, Grey. I'll get something cool to put on her head."

Grey scooped her up with ease, wending his way out of the bathroom and back into the living room, where he set her on the couch and Wanda put pillows under her head.

"What do we do?" Wanda fretted, folding and unfolding her hands. "How do we help her?"

Grey shook his head. He knew this was a normal occurrence for Sal, but for everyone around her, it was damn scary. "I don't know. If I recall correctly, she has to wake up on her own. She once told me Samantha always made sure she was tucked safely in bed with Buttercup by her side before she'd leave their apartment. But basically, she's just in a deep slumber. She's not hurting in any way."

"These visions—care to explain what exactly happens besides her passing out?" Heath asked, handing Grey a cup of strong black coffee.

Grey liked Heath. He appeared solid and trustworthy and very much in love with his beautiful wife. That he didn't say a word of protest about her involvement with this OOPS or all the danger she so selflessly put herself in made Grey admire him even more.

It took a strong man to let a woman pursue what gave her purpose when her purpose was so dangerous.

He liked Greg and Keegan, too. They'd all arrived today to check on their respective wives at the break of day, bringing their children with them. Both prepared to do whatever they could to help the Jeffersons.

Grey looked at Heath, his eyes grim. "I don't know a lot about them, to be honest. I know she has them and they're very real. Almost as though she's experiencing them, too. They take their toll on her, exhaust her, and obviously they're unpleasant at their best, terrifying at their worst. She's lost a lot of people in them. Some she knows, some related or affiliated with people she knows. It's a hard row to hoe. That much I can attest to after seeing the aftermath of the worst vision she's ever had."

"Poor baby," Marty said from the doorway. "What an awful way to live, with a constant dark cloud hanging over your head. I can't even imagine how she's suffered. It's no wonder she's not comfortable getting close to anyone."

Grey's head popped up. "How'd you know that?"

Marty scoffed at him in disapproval. "Is it really that hard to figure out? She lives alone, she grew up in the foster care system with Samantha as her closest ally. She felt like an outcast because of her ability, but at least she had Samantha. Now her friend's dead..."

"How do you know all this about her?" Grey asked.

Marty winked a fluffy eyelash. "Agent Carr is a lovely conversationalist whose affection for bacon makes his lips loose. Also, I wanted to know about her —where she came from, who raised her. So I asked. We all want to know about her, Grey, because she's an important part of the baby's world. I think we've said this before, Sal loved Samantha and that means something. It means she loves the baby, too. How could Wanda not want the baby to experience his mother through Sal? How could she not want Sal to experience Samantha's future though the baby?"

Then Wanda chimed in. "Look, for all our bickering and tussling, we're still a family. Or what Nina calls framily. We chose each other because we didn't have anyone else. We know what it feels like to be alone, and over the years, we've extended that framily and grown because we are so acutely aware of how that feels. That's why there's always room on the paranormal couch for one more with us."

Seeing Sal through Marty's and Wanda's eyes made him feel like more of an ass than ever before. He'd never focused on how she came to be the loyal warrior she was, only that she was indeed a warrior.

He'd never forget seeing her that day after her vision of Samantha dying. He'd never forget the wild terror in her eyes, the helpless, pleading horror of seeing her best friend's death. It had kept him up nights, and sometimes still did. Yet, he hadn't probed deeper about her past experiences with visions or considered the toll they must take.

But this vision she'd had today, he damn well hoped it was of the guy who'd fathered the Jeffersons' boy. He hoped the fuck rotted in an everlasting hell for killing Samantha—for the endless suffering he'd brought Sal.

Heath gripped his shoulder and asked, "If you think she'll be okay, can we talk about where we go from here? The guys and I have a loose plan, if you're willing to hear."

Damn, he liked these people. Their insight. Their unity. Their determination.

Grey nodded, just before he dropped a kiss on Sal's forehead and rose. "I'm willing to hear any and all plans, loose or otherwise. Carr and I are all ears."

"She's in good hands, Grey," Marty assured, settling down in the chair opposite the couch, pulling it close to the couch, and brushing a stray hair from Sal's forehead. "One of us will always be here with her until she wakes up."

As his chest tightened just looking at her so deeply asleep, he forced himself to head back to the dining room where they'd set up shop. He wanted to find this bastard.

And when he did, he'd hurt him for hurting Sal. If he never did another thing again, he'd make that mad motherfucker pay.

~

"Carl. Shhh, sweetie. She's still resting. But isn't she pretty?"

Sal heard Marty's voice from far away, forcing her

to dust the cobwebs from her mind and the haze of fog she suffered whenever she had a vision.

Oh, God. That vision. She couldn't think about it. Couldn't breathe from it. She forced it from her mind's eye and let her eyes flutter open to find who she assumed was Carl, staring down at her.

"Are you Carl?" she asked, her voice sounding gravelly from sleep.

He nodded, his face a light shade of green full of boyish charm just like the baby's. Then he grinned, wide, innocent, perfect. He was every bit what she'd been told. Shy, a little awkward, dressed like any other guy his age in slouchy jeans, a hoodie and high-top sneakers—whatever age that was.

Running his fingers over the duct tape at his wrists in a self-conscious gesture, he waved and said. "Hell...ooo, Ssal."

She smiled up at him, her eyes tearing at the corners because he was as sweet as everyone said. "Hello, Carl. It's so wonderful to meet you. Did you have a nice trip to your friend's ranch?"

"Yesss," he replied, reaching down to pat her shoulder before his hand brushed the side of her cheek. "Pretty."

Running a hand over her face, she smiled. "I bet I look a mess, but thank you, Carl. You're very sweet. Would you sit with me for a minute?" she asked, attempting to sit up, grateful she was waking up to a friendly face instead of alone on some cold floor. The way she usually woke up from the death scream these days.

Marty was beside her in a swirl of blonde hair and clanking silver bracelets. "Let me help. You sit with Carl and get to know each other and I'll get you some tea," she said on a warm smile.

As Marty sat her upright, her limbs typically weak from her vision, Carl sat beside her, his shy smile and bright eyes making her heart tighten and clench.

Clearing her throat, Sal asked, "Did you see the baby yet, Carl?"

He grinned wide, putting his hands in his lap. "Ba...byyy."

"He's perfect, isn't he? In fact, he's just like you."

Carl appeared satisfied with that. "Like me."

"Will you teach him everything you know?"

"Read. Yee...sss."

"You'll teach him to read, yes. Nina told me you love to read. Samantha would like that. She really would. She loved to read."

"Happy," he responded.

"Use your words, bud. All of them. You've got more than one," Nina said on a grin, entering the living room to take the chair Marty'd just left with a chubby, gorgeous dark-haired baby on her hip.

Carl beamed at Nina, making it clearer than clear she was his safe harbor, his rock, the person he most valued. What was clearest to Sal, if it hadn't been already, these people loved hard, fiercely, and the bonds they created with their offspring, be they biological or otherwise, were priceless.

"Read to...bay...babyyy. Like Charrrlie," he said, drawing out the words in slow fashion then smiling again.

"That's right. Just like you read to your sister Charlie. Carl's learning to read better and better every day, aren't you, buddy?"

"She's yours?" Sal asked, fascinated by the doll-like creature with eyes so like her mother's and hair caught up in a pink bow.

"This is Charlie. Our little miracle. Also my perpetually teething, wake-mommy-up-at-all-hours-of-the-afternoon, keeps-me-on-my-toes youngest. Isn't that right, you beast?" She rubbed noses with the baby, who gave her a gummy kiss followed by a gurgle of laughter.

That took her by surprise. She'd always thought vampires couldn't breed, and she said as much before she could catch herself. "But I thought vampires couldn't—"

"Looong story. Suffice it to say, it happened, and as much as I love kids, I don't ever want it to happen again unless there's morphine and a freakin' coma involved."

Sal laughed as Carl held out his hands and Charlie reached for him, her deep chocolate eyes sparkling. She tucked her chubby fist under Carl's chin and kicked her stout legs in excitement.

"She loves her big brother Carl more than all the

Cheerios in the world, don't you, Lovebug? Now." She looked to Sal. "We have things to handle."

Sal's stomach twisted into a knot. "Like?"

"Like that vision that left you flat on the floor. I think you shattered my flippin' eardrums, but we need to talk about it. So, Carl, you watch your sister for me, okay? And later we'll read to the baby and Charlie. I'm sure glad you're home, kiddo." She ruffled his hair and hitched her jaw to the kitchen—meaning, move it.

Sal rose, following behind Nina as though she were walking to her prison sentence, dragging her feet and slumping her shoulders.

Nina pointed to the chair at the wide island where Marty and Wanda sat, too. "So what did you see?"

Marty and Wanda both peered at her with expectant, perfectly made-up eyes, waiting.

Sal looked at the island's counter, keeping her eyes averted from their prying gazes. "I don't remember."

"Yeah. Nice lot of bullshit. Don't play with me, Sal. Tell us what you saw so we can help."

"You can't always help someone destined to die, Nina. That's not how it works. Sometimes, I don't even know the person. I drive myself crazy trying to piece together who's in a vision I've had and if it might end up being too late for them because I missed something. I live always wondering, if I'd put the puzzle together earlier, could I have saved them?"

Many times, she'd spent hours recreating her visions by drawing them, writing down specific things she remembered about the surroundings, seeing the faces of the victims over and over in her dreams.

There'd been a lot of things she'd like to have done in her life—maybe go to college, take a dance class, do something with her life rather than tend bar and dodge sloppy drunks. But bartending was about all she could handle mentally with the toll her dreams took.

Marty reached across the space between them and patted her hand. "Fair enough. Living like that, with the threat of death always breathing down your neck sucks. I don't know how you do it. But was the person in the vision someone you knew?"

She didn't want to talk about her vision. She just wanted to help keep the baby safe then go back to her life and try to pick up the pieces. "Why is that so important?"

Wanda's eyes were hesitant when she asked very calmly, "Was it one of us?"

She shook her head. "No! None of you. Swear it. Believe me, I'd tell you if I saw something like that, and I'd do whatever I could to prevent it."

"So these visions…they're not a sealed fucking deal? Like, fate or some shit?"

Sal looked at her hands. "No. Not always. There have been people I've warned and managed to keep out of harm's way. I guess in some cases it's fate. For instance, people who die of heart attacks or natural causes. But those visions are rare. Most of mine are… well, violent, I guess is the best word to describe them."

"Oh, honey. How awful," Wanda soothed, resting

her chin in her hand. "What a tough way to grow up. And you had no one to explain it to you?"

Shrugging her shoulders, Sal fought sharing too much about herself. She didn't want pity. Sure, she'd had a shitty childhood full of all the usual foster kid horror stories. Blah, blah, blah. No one wanted to hear about how hard her past had been. It was a total downer. She'd just come across as someone who hadn't learned to let go and move forward and worse, bitter. So bitter.

For all intents and purposes, she'd managed, and she'd keep right on managing.

So she brushed it off. "There were people who had advice. Sure. I had paranormal advisors who taught me how to keep things from humans and the like. But not another banshee. I've never met anyone else like me. I was in the human foster system, and back then, I wouldn't have even known where to look for another banshee because there was no Internet or social media. But that's neither here nor there. My interest is in helping keep you and the baby safe because I feel responsible—scratch that, I *am* responsible for bringing that man here. Also a top priority, catching this pig who...who hurt Samantha."

"So you don't know who your parents are?" Marty asked, her eyes full of sympathy.

Her gaze, so full of interest and understanding, made Sal uncomfortable. "Nope. I was abandoned. Both Samantha and I were."

Wanda dabbed at her eyes and said in a hushed tone, “I’m sorry.”

But she waved a dismissive hand. She’d been used to dismissing her abandonment since she was a kid. It only meant more probing and poking into her life she didn’t want to suffer. “I’ve lived with it for a long time. I’m used to it. Now can we get back to the business at hand?”

“Don’t be like that,” Nina ordered in a sharp tone, startling both her friends. “And don’t give me those big, wide-eyed, whaddya-mean-don’t-be-like-that looks. You know what I fucking mean. Don’t act like that shit didn’t affect you. It’s unhealthy.”

Marty flicked her fingers at Nina’s arm. “Dr. Statleon in da house! Look at you grow, Elvira. I’m so proud of you.” She tweaked Nina’s pale cheek and chuckled.

“Get the fuck off me, Overdone Barbie. I haven’t grown that much. Not enough to keep from kicking your ass if you don’t quit touching me.”

Grey poked his head into the kitchen, his handsome face stern and serious. He was so different as Agent Grey, compared to the Grey she’d gotten to know. But he still did things to her insides, and more than anything when she saw him, she wanted to go home, get in bed, pull the covers over her head and have a good cry.

“Ladies. I hate to break up the ass whoopin’, but I think we have an idea—maybe even a solid plan. We need to hash it out with you. Care to join us?”

They all rose at once, but Nina grabbed her arm and looked down at her, her coal-black eyes probing Sal's. "I meant what I said, dude. Don't pretend like that shit doesn't hurt or that it didn't happen. Of course your past hurts. Being lonely fucking hurts, kiddo."

Sal kept a straight face when she said, "When did you get your license to practice?"

Nina lifted her supermodel jaw, revealing her supermodel jawline. "You know, under normal circumstances, I'd just beat your ass for being a smart-mouth. But I used to do that to hide my reasons for being so angry when people can't be real. In light of that shit and all my self-discovery, I'm here to tell you, I'll still beat your ass, but it'll be to knock some sense into you. Grow a pair and address that you need love just as much as the rest of us. There's nothing wrong with it. And don't forget to work out your feelings about Agent Fifty Shades, either."

With that, Nina turned on her work boot and marched out into the dining room, leaving Sal to ponder her words.

Words that stung but also rang true. But it was all too much right now. Too much to digest.

Calamity, Nina's familiar, wound her tail around Sal's leg and purred. "She's a pain in the ass with all her find-yourself crap, isn't she?"

Sal laughed, kneeling down to scratch under the cat's chin. "She's pretty upfront."

"Christ, if you only knew. She's got all sorts of advice these days. She's forever analyzing me for one thing or another, and while I'm the first to tell you that I hate to admit it, she's usually right. We don't always want to hear the truth. It's human nature, Sal."

"Well, I'm not human," she offered flippantly, regretting the harsh tone to her voice.

"Deflect as much as you like, banshee. Can't hide from the truth. Now, on to more pressing matters—like your damn hound. Not a fan of her sniffing my ass. I realize it's a dog thing, but she's getting a little familiar with the familiar, if you know what I mean."

Sal barked a laugh, rising to her feet. "I'll certainly speak to her and tell her to knock it off."

"Appreciate it. Also, if there's ever a time you wanna sit down and talk about banshees, hit me up. I have a story or two to share. Might help you with a little insight into your origins in terms of history."

"Have you ever met a banshee?"

"Honey, have I met a banshee," she said saucily.

This information stunned her, but there was no time to delve deeper. The sooner they caught this guy, the better. "That would be awesome. Now, off to see a dog about some over-exuberant ass sniffing."

Calamity chuckled, swishing her tail as she exited the kitchen, leaving Sal alone with her thoughts.

A sigh of relief escaped her lips when she realized the women hadn't managed to pressure her about who'd she'd seen in her vision.

She wasn't ready to tell them—or to even face it herself.

She still had to parse where the hell she'd been in

that vision, make a list of the things she saw, recollect her surroundings and pinpoint identifying markers to try to prevent it from happening.

It behooved her to recall as much information as she could.

Because the person she saw dying in her vision was her.

CHAPTER 9

"Are you okay?"

"How do you define okay in your world, Agent Hamlin?" That was petty, and she knew it, but seeing him, interacting with him in a place where they'd once been so intimate, still stung her heart.

She didn't want to long for him. Need him. Wished things were different, but having to be so close to him made it impossible.

They'd decided to go back to her apartment so she could gather some personal things in case this sting they'd planned lasted longer than a couple of days. Until then, she'd stay with the Jeffersons. She'd never admit it, but she found herself thrilled to spend more time with these people and the baby, despite the ugly circumstances.

She liked their vibe—their overall network of ideas and as they'd bounced those ideas around, the ladies of

OOPS proving they sort of knew what they were doing when it came to a plan.

Grey sighed, grabbing the bag of her toiletries and hoisting it over his broad shoulder. "I'm sorry I lied. I hated it, but it was necessary to keep you safe, Sal. But just so you know, it made me feel like shit."

Her back to him, Sal stopped packing her overnight bag and shook her head even though she still wanted to crawl into her spring-popping bed, pull the covers over her head and hide.

Instead, she brushed off his words. "You shouldn't be. You were doing your job. You were doing the right thing, Grey. I'm the one who went too far when I looked at your private files. I can't be mad at you for trying to bust this trafficking ring wide open."

And she meant that. She'd have done whatever it took to find Samantha, too—even if it meant breaking up with Grey to get there.

Grey set her bag of toiletries on her bed and grabbed her hand, turning her around. "I meant everything I said when we were together."

"Which part do you mean? The part where you told me some guy in the future would be lucky to have me? Or the part where you told me you didn't want to commit to anything long term?"

Grey cupped her jaw and she found she didn't have the will to turn away. She was on very little sleep, leaving her feeling raw and vulnerable. But his eyes, those sexy eyes, scanned her face.

"That's not what I meant and you know it, Sal. What I meant was, I cared about you when we were together. I care about you now. But this investigation...I couldn't take a chance you'd end up in the middle of it."

Her snort was derisive as she fought the impulse to smooth the wrinkles in his black T-shirt. "And yet, here I am. In the middle of it. That's on me, and don't think I'm not accepting full responsibility for leading the horse to water. I brought this guy to the Jeffersons. I can't tell you how shitty I feel about that."

Saying it out loud to him didn't make her feel any less guilty, but she was intent on letting him know she knew he wasn't responsible just because he'd given her information he shouldn't have.

Grey's sigh was ragged. "If it makes you feel any better, he would have found them eventually. That's why we were watching them. He's desperate. If he doesn't produce the baby, they'll kill him, and it won't be quick. Better he's around sooner rather than later, when we'd moved on to some other facet of this mess. When we were still here to help."

"But his desperation's going to be our way in—or mine, anyway." The idea made her inwardly shudder with terror, but that wouldn't stop her. Nothing would keep her from seeing this fuck dead. And anything less than death wouldn't do.

"I'd do it, but I can only shift for a finite amount of time. If we run over, and I change back, he'll catch me. What we need to do is catch him in the act or we have no case with the exception of his assault on you, and you didn't even see him."

Her outrage grew every time she realized how this asshole had kept himself in the clear. "What about DNA? Wouldn't the baby be proof he'd forced Samantha to have a child? Essentially, he raped her, Grey! How can that not count for something?"

God, that word was so ugly. So hateful it made her want to crawl right out of her skin. Every time she thought about it, about how Samantha suffered, it was all she could do not to retch, rage, rail against the invasion of her sweet friend's person.

Grey's eyes went soft with sympathy. "Because we don't have Samantha here to testify and tell us as much. I hate to tell you this, but from the text messages, she appeared quite enamored. I think the sex could have been consensual. No, she didn't know what he really wanted. A baby to sell on the black market. She thought he wanted to be her boyfriend. But Samantha went willingly with him. Which brings me to this—so he fathered a child? Big deal in the eyes of the law, both paranormal and human."

That almost made her feel better. Almost. Clenching her fists, she insisted, "But I can prove she disappeared!"

"But can you prove he held her captive, Sal? Can you prove she didn't want to go with him? Can you prove he was the one who killed her? Where? When? How? There are texts that say she didn't disappear at all. She went willingly. Yet, those are the questions we need answered. We need proof he coerced her."

She was starting to see the dilemma he faced—*had* faced as he'd gotten further into his investigation.

"So we need irrefutable proof. Hardcore proof." And she was the bait.

"We do, and I'm going to tell you up front. I'm not crazy about this at all. Not at all. I stand by what the OOPS ladies said. It's crazy to be the bait."

Well, she wasn't exactly crazy about being a decoy either, but if it meant that bastard would leave the Jeffersons alone, and he'd pay for kidnapping Samantha and keeping her hostage, she'd do it.

On a deep breath, she said, "I'm going to be fine. He's human, Grey. It's not like he's a werewolf or vampire."

Running a hand through his hair, his jaw went hard. "And neither are you, Sal. You're a banshee. No special abilities. If something goes wrong, and you have to defend yourself…"

She grit her teeth. "I'll defend myself. I'm no weakling, Grey. I did grow up in a system where not everyone was kind to the kid who had screaming nightmares. There were plenty of reasons to put up my dukes. And I took some self-defense classes. My instructor said I have good reflexes."

"Did he say that as he was trying to talk you into sleeping with him?"

She smiled. Her instructor had been hot. "No. He said it over a caramel macchiato."

"Was he your boyfriend?"

"Why do you want to know?"

"Because as a one-time boyfriend, I know we say all sorts of things to get you to sleep with us."

She giggled. "You're a dirty dog, Grey Hamlin. The dirtiest."

Unexpectedly, he pulled her close, wrapping his arms around her waist, and as much as Sal didn't want to get sucked back into the warmth of his embrace, she relaxed against him. "We'll never be far when the deed goes down."

"Good enough."

"Is it?" he asked, the rumble of his words vibrating against her ear still pressed to his chest.

She closed her eyes and prayed she could walk away from him when this was all done. "It is. It's all we can do, Grey. If I'm the only way in, then I'm the only chance we have to keep the baby safe. I'll be okay."

Tilting her chin upward, he stared down at her, his eyes, once soft, now gone fiery. "I don't know what I'd do if something happened to you, Sal. I think I'd lose my mind," he whispered, before he pressed his lips to hers, capturing her mouth.

Her lips opened automatically, welcoming the slick slide of his tongue, the heat of his mouth. Her arms wound around his neck in a familiar response as they pressed against one another. Her heart sped up as her limbs wilted and she melted into him.

Her brain stopped functioning the moment he hauled her close and groaned against her mouth, reminding her of the nights they'd spent together while he'd looked for Samantha.

Sex had never been the problem. Opening up had—for both of them. Never once had she told him how she truly felt because she'd never felt like this before, and it frightened her. She felt all the things Samantha talked about having one day. A family, unconditional love. Support. Someone to snuggle with on a cold night. Someone's arm to hold when she entered a party.

As his hand grazed the underside of her breast, Sal moaned, pulling him tighter, clenching her eyes tight to keep her tears of longing at bay.

His phone sounded just as she was considering wiping her memory of the heartbreak he'd caused and giving in to her insatiable need to be as close as physically possible to him.

Grey pulled away on a harsh rasp, cursing softly as he pulled his phone from his pocket and barked a greeting into it.

Shaky and trembling, Sal turned away to finish gathering her things but her fingers didn't want to cooperate. Instead, as Grey talked to Carr, she headed to her kitchen with its yellow, chipped ceramic tile walls and peeling green linoleum.

As she compared it to Wanda's sprawling kitchen with gorgeous countertops and miles of cabinets, she reminded herself once again how much better off the baby was to have the Jeffersons. He wouldn't end up in this dumpy apartment for the rest of his life while she struggled to make ends meet.

She and Samantha had toyed with some DIY early on when they'd moved in, but resorted to painting and hanging some of her personal art because neither of them was very good with a hammer and nail.

But looking around at the space now, devoid of Samantha, she didn't much care about improving anything. It was just a one-bedroom dump with a dinky kitchen and a crumbling bathroom with a leaky faucet.

Pictures of their friendship siting on a shelf they'd actually managed to hang straight while they'd laughed and laughed, made her stop and stare. Samantha smiling at her next to the Christmas tree in Rockefeller Center, in particular, made her pause. Christmas had been Samantha's favorite holiday, and without fail, they always went to see the tree lighting.

Tracing her finger over the thick black frame, Sal gulped in a breath of air, fighting to keep from crying again. "I promise you, no matter what it takes, I'll keep him safe," she murmured.

"Did you take these pictures?" Grey asked from behind her, making her jump.

She lifted her shoulders, embarrassed. "I did."

"And the paintings and sketches on the walls? Yours, too?"

She was always uncomfortable telling people about her drawings. Some of them reflected the things she'd seen in visions. Almost an homage to the people she'd been unable to save. Sometimes, the sketches were of something in the vision that stood out and she'd hastily draw it in order to remember it as a clue. Later, she'd go back in and flesh them out, which also could help lead her to the person in the vision.

Samantha used to tell her it was a wall of memorials when Sal asked if she thought it was too maudlin to hang them.

"Yep. The paintings and sketches, too."

"They're beautiful, Sal. Why aren't you showing them in some gallery somewhere? Getting jobs as a photographer?"

"You mean as opposed to tending bar in a dive?"

"If you want straight shooting, yes."

"Because they're personal, I guess. They're some of the things I've seen in visions. I don't want to sell their pain. It feels wrong."

"But you draw other things, don't you? You're incredibly talented, Sal. I'd buy all of these."

There wasn't a lot of intimate, intimate details she knew about Grey other than his body. She'd fought hard not to get too close to him or let him too far into her world, even if she'd wanted to know everything about him. Finding he liked art was a small bit of him revealed.

Turning to face him, she asked, "Are you an art lover?"

"I'm an anything-that-shows-this-much-passion-and-heart lover."

She looked up at him thoughtfully and tilted her head. "I had no idea."

"There's plenty you don't know about me, Brice.

Plenty to learn."

"Really? Do tell," she mocked.

He smiled with a wicked grin. "I mean aside from the not-really-a-detective thing."

"How did you get involved in this agent thing anyway? Did you always want to hunt down our kind and put the bad guys away?"

"Good buddy of mine from college was killed in a drug bust by a bunch of werewolves. Quite by mistake. Wrong time, wrong place sort of thing, and I wanted to know what the hell happened. I asked a lot of questions around campus and the agency recruited me—mostly because of my ability to take another's form, but I passed the written exam with a reasonable score," he joked, but she knew the memory of his friend was painful.

Yet, she was surprised to find his situation was similar to the one she was in right now. "Did you catch the bad guy?"

His face went grim as he pushed his hands into the pockets of his jeans. "Got my ass handed to me, but yeah. Eventually, we caught the son of a bitch."

"Do you like what you do?"

"I do. It doesn't make for much of a life, but I promised myself when Jordy was killed, I'd do what I could to prevent another senseless death in his honor, and here I am, almost thirteen years later."

"Living the life of an international man of mystery?"

"If you call cold burgers on stakeouts and pretending to be a shitty detective mysterious, yep.

That's me. Veeery mysterious." He wagged an eyebrow at her and winked.

They'd inched closer to each other as they talked, but she didn't want a repeat of their earlier kiss. It would only be one thing more to miss about him when this was all over.

She took a step backward and asked, "Was that Carr on the phone?"

"Yep. We're ready for liftoff."

Her hands suddenly became clammy, but she forced herself to put on a brave face. "Then let's do this."

As she took one last look around her apartment, a thought occurred to her. She might never come back here again. Latching on to Grey's arm, she stopped him from heading toward the door.

"Hey, if anything happens to me, will you take Buttercup? I don't have anyone else, and I couldn't stand her ending up back in the shelter. She's a good girl. She deserves a good home."

"I think I'd have to fight the vampire for her. Do you really want to see me dead that badly?"

Sal laughed as she zipped up her bag and hauled it over her shoulder. "I'd pay good money to see that cage fight."

As they headed out the door, she impulsively grabbed a framed picture of her and Samantha in Central Park last fall, stuffing it into her purse.

This was for Samantha and the baby.

And she only had one chance to make things right.

God, please don't let me screw this up.

CHAPTER 10

"Vodka and cranberry," the awkward man, who looked more like a gangly teenager than a thirty-year-old at the bar, ordered, his New York accent thick.

He was exactly the type someone like Samantha had been drawn to. Someone a little socially awkward, not overly handsome, but boyishly blond and appealing enough to compensate with other attributes when necessary. "Funny-goofy" was the phrase Samantha had used in the texts between them Grey had showed her.

She'd read enough to know Samantha had indeed been enamored, and it killed her all over again to see how easily her friend had been fooled. She'd known Sam was hungry for more in her life—more than just the two of them and Buttercup—but she'd never have guessed just how desperate or how easily she could make this relationship the one thing, above all else, that she wanted most.

"You deaf? Vodka and cranberry. Like this year," he demanded, ordering the specified drink just like he'd said he would in the texts he'd unknowingly shared with Grey and Carr. It was her signal it was show time.

"I heard you. Good choice, by the way. Promotes a healthy urinary tract while fooling your liver into believing you care. Anyway, coming right up," Sal said, turning from him and forcing herself to composure.

This was the pig who'd murdered her best friend. The pig who'd forced her to—

Suck it up, Sal. Stay calm. Make the drink then make the offer. Make it good.

She busied herself pouring his drink, talking herself down off the ledge the whole way.

It was then Nina caught her eye at the end of the bar, wearing a ridiculous blonde wig that, while big and fluffy and very un-Nina-like, somehow didn't steal from her incredible beauty. She adjusted her black leather mini-skirt and red bustier and narrowed her eyes at Sal, reminding her of what she'd told her just a half hour ago.

"I'll fucking kill him if he so much as considers touching you, kiddo. I'll pull his shriveled dick through his belly button if he even twitches in your direction. I. Will. Light. That. Shit. Up. No fears. I got your back. Nobody's gonna hurt you. And if I don't get to that fuck first, Darnell will. You don't want to mess with this demon. He looks soft and GD squishy, but he's a fierce mothereffer."

She'd said all that as Marty applied so much lip gloss to Nina's lips she could stick them to a wall, as Wanda teased the vampire's shiny blonde wig and jammed her feet into some hot-pink stilettos.

Regardless of her outfit, there was no denying, Nina could wear almost anything and still be utterly gorgeous.

Marty and Wanda both paced the street in front of her workplace, each dressed as ladies of the evening, watching for any signs the big guys might show up instead of Samantha's murderer. As comical-looking as Nina, they played the part to perfection as Marty popped her gum and her big hoop earrings swayed while she walked, and the ultra-conservative Wanda hoisted her breasts upward to achieve the best cleavage.

Heath, Greg, and Keegan all leaned against the brick façade of the bar, just by the dirty picture window with the neon "open" sign blinking, looking like a motorcycle gang as they threw back beers and openly leered at their women.

They, too, had told her the man in question would welcome death should he harm a single hair on her head.

Sal kept repeating those words to reassure herself as she watched Darnell spin around on a sticky barstool, a big, sweet teddy bear, pretending to be Nina's pimp.

Dressed in what he'd dubbed his pimp-rapper look, complete with thick gold chains, long leather trench coat, and his infamous high-top gold sneakers, it was all Sal could do not to laugh out loud.

He waved a finger at Nina. "Gurrrll, why ain't you out on that damn street makin' me some money, 'stead a in here actin' like you ain't gotta work for a livin'? This ain't no free ride. Shoot. Light bill ain't gonna pay itself, girl," he said to the vampire as he took a sip of his non-alcoholic beer and leered at her.

And he was good at it, too. Almost too good. So good, Sal virtually had to fight off a rash of giggles.

As she slid the drink toward the man who'd brutally robbed her friend of her future, one Bradley Simmons, she leaned forward and said the words he was waiting to hear. "I'm Sal Brice. You know, the woman you hit over the head with a baseball bat? Wanna make some money?"

He leaned forward on the bar, his arms sticking to the surface as he grabbed at a bowl of peanuts and took a handful as though they weren't talking about stealing a baby and selling it to these freaks he was in business with.

Neither Carr nor Grey nor even the agency they worked for were sure how a human like Bradley had gotten himself mixed up in paranormal trafficking. It astounded them as much as it had the ladies of OOPS to know a human knew of their existence. They were only interested in getting on the inside and working their way to the top of this ring of paranormals to end this heinous practice.

She'd heard rumblings of conversations about the adoption agency possibly being involved, but they had no definitive answers at this point.

He snapped his fingers in her face. "Hey. How the fuck am I supposed to be sure you're not a cop or the Feds?"

Leaning forward, she cupped her chin in her hand and gave him a far saucier smile than she though herself capable. "I guess you'll just have to take your chances if you want a baby to sell. That's how the fuck you're supposed to know."

His sharp jaw lifted and his eyes narrowed. "Are you one of them?"

"One of who?"

"A fucking zombie like Samantha."

"Nope. Not a zombie or a werewolf or a vampire or whatever the hell else is out there."

"Jesus, the shit I've seen since I got all wrapped up in this thing... I mean, since Samantha."

She didn't want to know. Didn't want to hear. She couldn't hear or she'd yark all over the front of his plaid shirt.

So she flipped up her middle finger. "Fuck Samantha!" she spat, using every bit of her self-control not to vomit as she spoke the words. "Damn whiner. Always whining about wanting a boyfriend, a family. It's all bullshit. I give as much shit about her as I do you. I just want the money. You'd have known that if you'd given me a chance to tell you before you clobbered me, douchebag."

"I thought you were her best friend."

Sal laughed derisively, tamping down the acrid bile rising in her throat. "She thought so, too."

"Christ, you're a cold bitch."

Drumming her fingers on the bar top, she cocked her head. "And you have a warm heart? Aren't you selling your own damn kid?"

Bradley didn't bat an eye—didn't even flinch with one iota of guilt. "Whatever. Let's get down to the reason for this meet. Look, how are you gonna get your hands on the kid?"

Sal made a face at him. "Did you not see me in there, working those morons—in their own house, mind you—like a pro before you whacked me? I gave them a sob story about being Samantha's BFF and how I wanted to be a part of the baby's life because of her. She'd want it that way—sold them the whole bill of goods. Blah, blah, blah. They fell for it hook, line, and sinker. Said all the right things, just like I did with Samantha."

He sat back and used his palms to straighten his arms as he looked at her skeptically. "She said you've been friends since you were fucking kids. You played her all this time?"

Sal flapped a hand at him, dismissing the notion. "Samantha was delusional. She was always creating shit in her head that didn't exist. Sort of like her relationship with you."

Grey and Carr had said if she kept her explanations simple, it was easier to remember later if she had to recall it, and then Nina had told her not to shoot for an Academy Award her first sting.

Bradley took a swig of his drink before he said, "She always said so much nice shit about you. You kinda suck."

"I wouldn't go pointing the suckage stick so fast, asshole. Are you forgetting you became a baby daddy just so you could make some cash? Now, you wanna hear the rest of this, or do you want to reminisce like some pussy?"

He rolled his hand in the air. "Carry on."

"So I show up tomorrow at their house and ask to take the baby for a walk. You meet me at the end of the street, we disappear with the baby, give it to whoever the fuck you give babies to when you're selling them, and we split the cash sixty-forty. I'm the sixty, by the way."

"How the fuck did you find them, anyway? It took me three days to track that kid down."

She shrugged arrogantly. "I know people who know people. How the fuck did you lose the baby to begin with?"

"Somebody damn well stole him from me, that's how!" he growled, slamming his hand against the bar.

"Who?"

Bradley's lips thinned. "That's none of your damn business. She's been taken care of."

Fighting a shiver, Sal pushed for the words she so

longed to hear. "So do we have a deal or what? I don't have all day. I, unlike you, who shoots his sperm once and makes a couple million bucks, have a job." She spread her arms wide to indicate the dark cavern of the bar with its littered floor and cracked jukebox. "Now do we have a deal?"

"Fuck your sixty."

"Fuck your forty," she said, hitching her jaw. "You want an easy way to get the baby; I'm your girl. You wanna find a way into that fortress with those lot of viper bitches, good luck. I'll still have a job. You'll be dead because whoever the fuck you promised this baby to is probably pretty pissed right now."

She purposely turned her back on him, throwing her towel over her shoulder and behaving indifferently. As she did, she caught sight of herself in the worn mirror above the bar, her cheeks red, her chest heaving as she gulped in breaths of the stale air.

"Fuck," he mumbled. "Hold up now."

Turning around slowly, she plastered a catty smile on her face and raised an eyebrow in question, crossing her arms over her chest without saying a word.

"Fine. You get sixty." He held out his hand to shake on it.

But she wrinkled her nose and waved his hand away. "Winner-winner-chicken-dinner."

"God you're a cold-hearted bitch. You're nothing like Samantha said you were."

"I'm betting you're nothing like she thought you were in the end either, are you? I told you, Samantha lived in a fucking fantasy world, is what Samantha did. So who's cold-hearted? Her mourning best friend or the freak human who digs making babies and selling them to the highest bidder?"

He looked her up and down with an appraising glance and grinned. "Bet you're wicked in bed. A real wild one. Shoulda hooked up with you instead."

Sal played along, sending him a flirty smile while running a playful finger along his arm. "Fat chance you'll ever find out. No way your skinny, awkward ass would get close enough to knock me up then kill me when I was done breeding for you, freak boy."

His face got real close to hers when he asked, "Who says she's dead?"

Sal's eyebrow rose. "Who says she's not? Who gives a shit if she's not?"

He didn't blink once at her callous words. "Oh, yeah. She told me you see shit. Did you see her die? Is that how you found my kid?"

"Nuh-uh-uh," Sal taunted, wagging her finger. "Don't you worry about how I found the kid or you. Worry about how you're going to sleep at night, knowing you created a baby for the sole purpose of selling it, freak boy."

He pushed off from the stool, his face red with anger as he seethed, "Fuck you and your judgment."

Maybe she'd gone too far? Shit! But she couldn't turn back now. She had to continue this callous, greedy act or she'd lie down on the floor and cry her eyes out right before she punched him in the face. "I'll see your fuck you and raise you your head on a platter."

His face went tight and hard, and for a brief second, she wished Samantha could have seen that expression, just once, instead of the goofy, charming face he wore when he'd walked into the bar.

But she'd pushed for a reason. It was her passive-aggressive stab at him for murdering her best friend. She also knew his life was in danger because he hadn't produced the baby, and he knew it, too—which meant he'd do whatever she said in order to get the baby.

"Tomorrow. Five o' clock. Meet me at the end of Sunshine Lane or whatever the fuck they call it over there in Happy Land."

"As long as you have the cash at the meet. Otherwise, no go. I'll hand that kid back over to Susie Sunshine faster than you can say freak sperm donor. Got it?"

Leaning into the bar, his face went from boy next door to mask of evil terror. "Fuck off, bitch," he seethed.

Sal didn't even blink. Rather, she smiled and winked. "See ya tomorrow, freak." Waving her fingers, she left the bar area and headed for the back hall where the bathrooms were located.

Leaning against the grimy wall covered in graffiti, Sal closed her eyes and began to shake all over—full-body, violent shivers. Tears streamed down her face as she silently begged Samantha to forgive her for the horrible things she'd said about her.

She felt dirty, filthy, sick with the scum she'd just bandied with as though she did things like this every day. Disgust washed over her in wave upon wave of ugly heat, engulfing her, dragging her into the dark abyss of horror.

And then Grey was there, wrapping his strong arms around her and pulling her close. He whispered soothing words she didn't hear as she sobbed her anguish against his shoulder until she was dry, and the only thing that remained was this soul-numbing grief.

~

"Susie Sunshine?" Wanda asked with a laugh, her face now devoid of much more than lip gloss and mascara, her hair back up in a messy bun.

Sal tucked the sweater around her shoulders and gave her a sheepish wince from across the big farm-style table. "I'm sorry. I didn't mean it. But the longer the conversation went on, the easier it became. I just sort of got into it and before I knew it, I went all Meryl Streep."

Carl reached over and pulled her into an awkward hug then patted her on the back. "Gggood. Youuu are gggood," he said.

Sal smiled at him, suddenly shy at all this praise she didn't deserve.

Nina nudged her with a flat palm to her back and cackled. "No shit. Though, I kinda like viper bitches. It has a definite ring to it."

"Sorrysorrysorry!" she cried out again, forgetting that part of the conversation she'd had with Bradley. "I don't know what came over me. I was never even in a school play and all of a sudden it was just happening. I was threatening him and cussing a blue streak, taunting him, calling him names. I'm sure I sounded like a bad impression of Gemma Teller from *Sons of Anarchy*."

"You were amazing, young lady," Heath praised, lifting his wine glass of blood to salute her. "Bravo!"

"Hear-hear!" Carr chimed in.

"How do you know? You were outside pretending to be a biker thug with the rest of your thug gang," Sal protested on a giggle, squirming in her seat.

Heath pinched the tip of his earlobe and grinned. "Vampire hearing. I can always hear you now."

Turning to her left, Sal looked down the table at Darnell, who sat next to Greg and Keegan. "And you? The light bill? The light bill ain't gonna pay itself?" she mimicked his earlier rendition of rapper-pimp. "You, sir, were brilliant!"

Darnell brushed his shoulders and sniffed before he laughed. "It ain't nothin' but a thing."

"You were amazeballs, Sal. Don't you ever think otherwise," Marty praised with a wink. "And I was thinking, too bad our resident vampire doesn't show up in pictures after wearing that outfit. Hashtag laughs for days, people!"

The resident vampire flipped her friend the bird before turning to Grey. "And whaddaya have to say about our girl here, Agent Fifty Shades?" Nina prodded. "She's one helluva actress, huh? Maybe you guys should think about hiring her for keeps."

Grey's smile was warm when he looked into her eyes, furthering her discomfort. "She was brilliant. I'm quite impressed."

Nina gave her a shove with her hand. "And the sixty percent shit? Fuck, kiddo. You got some set on ya. Just swingin' 'em all over the joint, wild and free."

Everyone laughed but Sal suddenly sobered, swallowing hard as she played with the edges of her cloth napkin. "We still have to catch him."

Nina scoffed, her face full of distaste. "Oooh, we'll catch the freaky-deaky fuck. Worry not, my little Academy Award nominee. And when we do, all I ask is two minutes alone with him. Just two. We'll see how hard he's swinging that dick when I'm rippin' it off him and shoving it down his skinny, smug throat."

Archibald rested a hand on her shoulder as he took her plate. "I daresay, Mistress Sal. I'm ever so sorry I missed this adventure, but the fair maidens in charge assured me no one would take me seriously as a pimp. Imagine my surprise when they told me I wouldn't fit the part with my uppity British accent and my elegant lines. How are they to know whether I can wear gold chains and feathered hats? Discrimination, I say! I feel an ageism complaint going into that suggestion box," Archibald teased as he began clearing the rest of the dinner plates.

Sal laughed again before offering to help clear the

dishes, but Archibald refused, clicking his heels and shaking a finger. "Absolutely not! I heard the tape of your performance today and anyone who can spit in the face of danger the way you did, stare it right in the eye without flinching, knowing this was the man responsible for such a heinous deed, does not do dishes. Not on this manservant's watch! You shall rest and possibly have another piece of coconut cake, yes?" He wiggled his eyebrows at her, making her smile.

She felt so spoiled. Archibald had made the most amazing meal Sal could remember having since...well, never. He'd asked what her favorite food was just before they'd left to meet with Bradley, and she'd stumbled.

She'd existed on Twinkies and tuna sandwiches bought at the gas station for so long, she couldn't remember. So she'd asked him for comfort food—food to heal the soul.

And he'd provided by making batches of crispy, juicy fried chicken, an amazing gruyere-and-bacon macaroni and cheese so creamy and cheesy, her cholesterol fairly begged her not to take another bite, with saucy baked beans and buttery corn on the cob.

As she sat back and watched everyone interact as though they shared meals like this often, her heart constricted and she found it difficult to swallow.

This was what Samantha had craved, family gatherings, laughter, love, and she supposed, it was what she craved, too.

When this was over, she'd miss this—miss something she'd only experienced for a couple of days, yet had made an impression so rich and textured, it would last her a lifetime.

She caught Grey's eyes, and he smiled at her from across the table, and then she remembered he'd be gone after tomorrow, too. Likely off chasing the big guys in charge of this trafficking case, and that was when the emptiness hit her, making her excuse herself from the table to use the bathroom.

As she made her way upstairs, she heard the baby cooing softly in his crib and poked her head inside his bedroom.

Wow. His room shouldn't have been a surprise to her, compared to the rest of the house, but the detail, the love, the caring put into it showed.

The walls, done in soft grays and various shades of blue accents, instantly calmed her. In the middle of it all was the baby's crib, a testament to someone's woodworking talents. Painted a light whitewashed gray to accent the walls, it had the kind of ornate scrollwork she'd only seen on some of those fixer-upper shows made by expert woodworkers.

Colorful bumpers with rocket ships and stars padded the crib and a hanging mobile with astronauts and moons in their various phases hung above him, softly tinkling a sweet lullaby. A changing table stocked full of diapers and wet wipes and tiny clothes for him sat under the window beside a rocking chair.

But the wall behind his crib made her pause and

catch her breath. There hung a thickly framed picture with a poem that gripped her heart.

Not flesh of my flesh.

Nor bone of my bone.

But still miraculously my own.

Never forget for a single minute

You didn't grow under my heart,

But in it.

Fleur Conkling Heyliger

Leaning over the crib, she peeked down at him, swaddled in a crocheted blanket, and ran a finger down along his soft cheek as her eyes filled with tears. "Oh, little guy. I hope you always know how important you are to these people. How much they loved you before they even knew you. I hope you grow big and strong and turn into a man just like your father. Brave and kind, warm and welcoming. You're such a lucky, lucky boy."

Wanda came in behind her, leaning her arms on the crib beside Sal's. "I hope he knows how lucky *we* feel. I feel like he's always been with me—even when he was screaming up a blue streak."

"I think he was meant to be with you. This was a win all 'round in my eyes."

"But don't think for a second he won't get all kinds of discipline. I've heard sometimes, adoptive parents go overboard and overcompensate with toys and allow poor behavior because they never want the child to feel like he's anything different than their own. I don't understand that guilt, and maybe that's because in one sense or another, we've all sort of adopted one another, but I'll not have a spoiled boy. He'll learn respect as much as he'll learn love."

Sal smiled down at the baby, now drifting off to sleep, his eyelids lightly veined beneath his skin. She'd longed for those things as a kid, too. He wouldn't always be happy about discipline, but someday he'd know it was for his own good.

She looked up at Wanda. "You're going to be the best mother ever."

Wanda's eyes grew teary. "Ya think? I'm terrified to do something wrong. I think I've read every parenting book ever published because of it. And lately, I'm sappy and emotional. I'm tired and stressed out, but one thing I am is determined to get this right because what if this is my only shot to be a mother? How do I know they'll let me adopt more babies? Maybe we just got lucky."

Sal nodded her head, tucking her hair behind her ears. "I think you'll figure it out. I *know* you'll figure it out, no matter how many children you adopt."

"Will you help me—us?"

Keeping her eyes down, flattered beyond flattered, she whispered, "I wish someone like you had adopted me all those years ago."

She'd always wondered what just one good, kind person could have done to change her childhood, but it wasn't meant to be and she'd accepted that as she grew older.

Wanda nudged Sal's shoulder with hers and chuckled. "Well, technically, you're adopted already whether you like it or not, you know. It's never too late to find a family. So don't think you can get away from this pieced-together one that easily."

"You're the nicest person I've ever met, Wanda, and I mean that."

Grinning, she cupped her chin in her hand as she rubbed the baby's back. "Really? Usually everyone says Nina's the nicest person they've ever met. Score one for me."

Sal had to cover her mouth to keep from barking a laugh and startling the baby. "Thank you for being so gracious to me—letting me stay here while this goes down. I did something pretty shady to all of you by deceiving you, but I promise you, I'll make it right. I'll make sure this guy Bradley goes away forever."

"Oh, I dunno. I don't think it was shady at all. I think it was inspired and harmless and very brave, with us lot ready to pounce on a dime. But most of all, I think it was done with more love than you're comfortable expressing aloud just yet. But we'll show you how. How can I ever be mad at that?"

On impulse, she gripped Wanda's hand and squeezed it, inhaling her floral scent. It was the closest thing to words of gratitude she could manage.

Wanda patted her hand and grinned in understanding. "Now, last I heard, there was a second piece of cake waiting for you downstairs. We've already disappointed Arch once today by not letting him get his pimp on. We don't want to do that again by snubbing his culinary delights, do we? He can be an ornery, dare I say a spiteful British SOB."

She giggled and looked into Wanda's eyes. "Well, we can't have that, can we? Cake it is."

Sal took one last glance at the baby before she left him to be with Wanda, her heart full, her determination sealed.

If everything went wrong tomorrow, she'd spent an incredible couple of days with some amazingly giving people.

It more than made up for a lifetime of doing without.

CHAPTER 11

Grey peered down at Sal and gripped her shoulders, his stomach tied into a tight knot. "Okay, so you're sure you know what to do, right? We've got to get him on tape saying he's selling the baby. Forget the other stuff about Samantha for the moment. I know you hate that, but we still have no physical proof he killed her. We do have proof he wants to sell a baby. Stick to the plan, okay? Promise me you'll stick to the plan. No variations. Please."

She pressed her fingers to her ear, obviously to be sure the earpiece he and Carr so carefully fitted her with was in place. They could hear everything and she could hear them, he'd reassured himself.

Inhaling deeply, she nodded with a sharp bounce of her beautifully glossy black head. "I promise."

"No fancy talk, no goading him this time, as good as you are at it. In and out. That's it," Grey insisted, his jaw tight and hard.

"Got it," she replied, wiping her hands on her jeans and shivering, even though it was a beautiful seventy-two degrees in suburbia today.

"I'd go if I could, but I don't know how long I can last," Grey repeated for the hundredth time since this morning out of sheer guilt. Christ, she looked so small and fragile he wanted to haul her off somewhere safe and lock her up.

She licked her dry lips and gripped his wrists. "I know you can only skinwalk for a few minutes at a time. I get it. Don't sound so guilty, Grey. If it goes sideways, it's better he not catch you or we'll lose him forever. I won't let that happen. Please, it's going to be okay."

"And Calamity will be in the bushes. If he tries anything, she'll whip up a spell or something," Marty reassured, pressing a kiss to her cheek and giving her ponytail a tug.

"I'll zap that tool so fast, he'll shit himself," the cat reassured, winding her tail around Sal's legs. Grey had never met a familiar before, but she'd prove invaluable as a spy.

"We're on in ten!" Carr called from the dining room.

That was the moment his stomach took a nosedive and he had to swallow several times to keep from upchucking his heart.

"Out of the way, Fifty Shades," Nina crowed, shoving him aside. "You can slobber all over her when this is done."

Grey took a step backward as Nina pulled Sal into a hug and ran her knuckles over her scalp. "You go shit all over his day, kiddo. If he twitches the wrong way, he'll have the men and me all up in his shiz, okay? Now breathe, Banshee. Just breathe."

She buried her face in Nina's hoodie for only a moment before she whispered, "Okay, Marshmallow."

"Shut the fuck up, Screamer," Nina said back, setting Sal away from her with a grin and a final warning. "Be safe."

As the hive of activity buzzed around them and Sal prepared for the meet with Bradley, as each woman hugged her hard, Grey knew he had to take the opportunity to at least tell her he wanted more—from her, for them.

Pulling her to the front entryway where a carriage with a fake baby lie, swaddled and partially covered, he cupped her chin, letting his fingers roam her silky-soft skin. "When this is done, can we talk?"

She appeared genuinely perplexed as her wide round eyes met his. "About what?"

"About us." There. He'd said it, and it felt good.

"I thought you didn't want an us?"

"You thought wrong, Sal. That was only to protect you and keep you out of this mess. It was hard enough worrying one of these pukes would find you when you were asking all those questions about Samantha. Me and every informant I had on this case thought we'd made it a point to send out the message you knew nothing. I thought you were safe from them, from him—"

"Until I blew it by showing up here and basically handing him every answer he needed on a silver platter because I just couldn't listen."

"I'll say it one last time, that's not on you. It's on my poor agenting and me. I should have locked those damn files up. But there's nothing I can do about that damn mistake now. As much as I want to catch this fuck, I want you more, Sal. I want *you,* and I want you to consider getting to know Grey the agent, Grey the man."

She appeared to assess that for a moment before her face lightened a little. "I'd like that."

He smiled down at her, soaking up every inch of her beautiful face. "Good. Now let's go catch us a freak." Pulling her toward him, he planted a soft kiss on her lips before letting her go.

As she knelt and wrapped her arms around Buttercup's broad neck and gave her a squeeze, then took the handle of the baby carriage and headed out the door, his chest tightened at the sight.

She's gonna be okay, Hamlin. You and Carr are some of the best at what you do. This is a tight plan. She'll be okay.

~

Sal pushed the baby carriage down the sidewalk, breathing in and out to keep her nerves at bay. It was going down just like Grey said.

Simple, light, quick. No Academy Award performances tonight.

Rounding the corner, she caught sight of the prick. He leaned up against a beat-up gold Volvo, his ankles crossed, his apparel casual in jeans and a light pullover sweater in periwinkle blue, looking just as gawky-charming as he had the other day.

"I've got eyes on you, Sal. Nice and steady now, and remember, all we need to do is get him to incriminate himself by saying he's going to sell the baby—or any derivative thereof."

She gave a slight nod to her head to acknowledge Grey in her ear, but her white-knuckled grip on the carriage with the fake baby was a sure indication she was petrified.

The sun shone warm and bright as it began to lower in the sky, putting a glare on everything surrounding Bradley. Damn, she should have worn sunglasses.

Growing ever closer to him, she tried to focus on the words Grey had said instead of the whir of activity his words had stirred in her head. He wanted to talk, and the impression she got was he wanted to pursue a relationship.

The idea both scared and thrilled her, but she knew it was what she wanted, too—probably more than anything other than keeping the baby safe. Now if they could just catch this bastard and find a way into this trafficking ring, they just might have a shot.

"Well, well, five o'clock on the dot," Bradley drawled with a sneer. "I like a bitch who's on time."

Cupping one hand over her eyes to block the sun, she stayed far enough away to keep the carriage from getting too close, putting herself between him and the baby so he couldn't get a closer look.

"Shut your mouth!" she whisper-hissed, flashing her angriest eyes at him as she pretended to be afraid someone would hear them. "You'll wake him, and you don't want to hear this kid squalling like a damn banshee. Your ears will ring for days. Now, I don't have the time or inclination to bullshit-banter with you today. Cough it up."

"Cough what up?" he taunted, leering at her.

Her hand tightened on the handle of the carriage, but then that thing happened to her. The same thing that had happened in the bar—the thing where she became someone else entirely.

"Listen, freak boy, I will turn this bitch around and hand the kid right back to 'em. Either let's get it on or blow the fuck off, because my time's precious."

He threw up two hands like white flags and chuckled as though amused at her ire. "Stay in your lane already. Jesus, you're a bitch."

Lifting her chin in haughty disdain, she shot back, "And you're a pervert. Whatever. Where's this going?"

"It's going exactly where we said it would go in that damn dump you work in."

"Take it easy, honey," Grey whispered in her ear, his soothing tones easing her nerves a bit. "Coax him nicely."

Slowly, gently, she reminded herself. "And do you

remember what I said in the bar? I'd like you to remind me so we're clear, because if you gyp me…"

Bradley's face went hard as he popped open the door to the rusty Volvo. "Sixty-forty is what we agreed on."

"We need him to say it's for the sale of the baby. Pick the baby up and keep him close to your chest so he can't see him. Remind him what he's getting for his forty, Sal," Grey instructed with a hard edge to his tone.

She did exactly as Grey instructed, leaning forward, her eyes never leaving Bradley, and scooping the baby up. Sal pointed at the bundle in her arms. "Here's your forty, show me my sixty or I'm not handing him over."

Pulling a worn blue duffel bag from the car, Bradley popped it open to show where wads of cash sat, just waiting, and gave her a smug look.

"He needs to confirm the money's in exchange for the baby, Sal," Grey warned, ratcheting up her pulse.

Fuck! How was she going to get him to say it out loud? "How the fuck do I know you're not bullshitting me? How can I be sure it's all there?"

He held up the bag and shook it at her. "Does it look like a bag of cash, for Christ's sake?"

She backed away, cuddling the fake baby close to her breast. "Easy there, buddy. Don't get hinky with me. I'm just trying to do the same thing you are—get ahead in this life. I'm checkin' all my boxes, is all. So let's do this, you toss the money by my feet, I give you the package."

Bradley shook his summery blond head and

clucked his tongue at her in mock disapproval. "Um, no. Do you think I'm some kind of idiot? We both put them on the ground together and switch off."

She gasped and tsked by clucking her tongue back at him. "I'm a bitch, but I'm not so much of a bitch I'd put a harmless baby on the ground, asshole. Jesus, I can't believe you have the means to reproduce."

His face went all shades of red with frustration as he spat, "Goddammit, you fucking pain in the ass, I have the money for him, now give me the baby! He's *my* friggin' kid!"

"Like taking candy from a baby!" Grey shouted in her ear. "We got him, honey!" He paused for a mere second before she heard, "Carr, where the hell are you? Where's the…? Aw, fuck! Jesus Christ, find Carr, dammit!"

Frowning, she didn't know what to do next until everything happened at once.

The fake baby was ripped from her arms as someone steamrolled her right at the waist, knocking her so hard, Sal was sure her insides were now on the outside and she'd never breathe right again.

Then she heard Grey screaming something in her ear, Calamity summoning some kind of spell, and Nina pounding out of the bushes from across the road with a roar—but those were the last things she heard before someone put a hand covered with a cloth over her mouth, and she passed out.

CHAPTER 12

Sal woke with a long groan, her chest and abdomen so tender, she almost couldn't breathe. As what happened back at the Jeffersons began to register, the images racing through her mind, she fought a sob.

She'd been trampled by something huge and snarling, and to say whatever it had been had probably broken a few ribs in the process was an understatement.

Rolling over, she inhaled a mouthful of dirt. Spitting it out with a hacking cough, she attempted to sit up, but it hurt like hell to move on the hard surface. Instead, she curled into a ball and listened—just listened to the sounds around her, sniffing the air to get a sense of where she'd landed.

Her ear cocked as she silently tried to talk herself into getting up, but she heard nothing except a dull thud on occasion. Otherwise, it was silent as a tomb and frankly, just as dark.

Using the palms of her hands, Sal moved them around, grabbing handfuls of dirt as she felt her way across the floor with the span of her arm, and that was when she hit a solid wall of rock.

Everything in that moment stopped for her. She stopped breathing, stopped feeling, went totally numb as her body went ice cold with shivers of fear.

Slow your roll, Brice. Think. Slow down and think before you panic. Try and remember what happened before someone plowed you down and rearranged your lungs.

"Grey," she croaked. Grey had been talking her down, keeping her on an even keel as she tried to get Bradley to admit he was selling the baby.

But then he'd screamed something in her ear just before she'd been tackled, something about finding Carr.

No. No, they couldn't have gotten to Carr, could they? He'd been with the baby. He'd sworn he'd stay with him in case Bradley brought help to try to snatch the baby. But Bradley had been alone. She'd seen no one but him. Yet, truth be told, the sun had been in her eyes and it was hard to see everything. *Oh, God. Please don't let anything have happened to the baby!*

Fighting a sob, Sal stuffed her fist in her mouth to keep from crying out. It would do no one any good if she started losing her shit.

Walking her hands up the wall, the rough surface scratching at her palms, she managed to sit up and pull her knees to her chest, alleviating the pain in her ribs a bit, allowing her to think more clearly.

Where the hell was she? And how the hell had someone as scrawny as Bradley knocked her down like a wrecking ball?

"Hellloooo, down there!" a cheerful but muffled voice from above her head called.

Her eyes swung upward to where the voice sounded like it came from. "Hey! What the hell is going on?" she bellowed, her throat scratchy and sore, and why did she recognize that voice?

"Hey, Sassy Pants! Don't be so demanding. I'll tell you when I'm good and ready," the voice taunted playfully, just as the sound of something heavy shifting above her creaked and a flashlight shone down on her, so bright it hurt her eyes, revealing where she was.

As her eyes adjusted, her heart went into overdrive and her hands went clammy. Attempting to rise to her feet, she took a good look around and fought the rise of total terror.

This had to have been how Samantha felt. Alone, cold, terrified of her fate, and it was all Sal could do not to scream with the pictures she couldn't stop creating in her mind.

And then, someone stuck their head in front of the light. "So, my little actress, what do you have to say for yourself now? You've got quite a conundrum, don't you? How are you feeling by the way? I get carried away sometimes and don't always know my own strength. Did I break anything when I took your sweet ass out? An ass that's going to bring me a nice fortune, by the way. So are you hurt? Please say yes."

Forcing herself to look up, Sal saw for the first time who'd steamrolled her—and then everything made sense.

But more than putting this mess together, more than knowing the answer to the questions Grey had about this elusive trafficking ring, she realized something else.

This pit, this dark, dirty hole in some ground somewhere, the walls rife with despair, was what she'd seen in her vision.

This was where she was going to die.

~

"What the fuck just happened out there?" Nina screamed in his face, her eyes flashing all manner of hatred in his direction as she poked him in the chest. "You'd better fucking fix this, Agent Fifty Shades, or I'm going to eat you alive!"

Fuuuck! It was all Grey could do not to put his fist through a wall. That son of a bitch. That motherfucking son of a bitch!

Wanda approached him with Heath hot on her heels, her face riddled with anguish he almost felt, it was so raw. "He has the baby! *The baby*. Do you hear me, Agent Grey? He has my baby!" she shrieked, her entire body shaking with violent tremors.

Heath gripped her arms and forced her to look at

him. "Honey, listen to me—listen!" he demanded, shaking her with gentle force to bring her back into focus. "We will find the baby. I will find the baby, and then I'll take care of business. Please, hear me. I will find our son."

Her breath shuddering in and out, Wanda nodded as Marty rushed to her side and dabbed at the tears sliding down Wanda's face. "We'll find them, Wanda. Oh, honey, don't cry. Please don't. We'll find him and when we do, I'll help Nina eat his face off."

Nina wrapped her arms around Wanda and Marty and squeezed them both, but her next words, though said with love, were stern. "Wanda, knock this shit off right now. We need your head in the game. You feel me? In the game. Get yourself together and let's find this motherfucker."

Wanda nodded and gulped for air as Grey fought to keep his head on his shoulders and do his job rather than dwell on the biggest betrayal he'd ever experienced.

"Everyone, listen up!" he shouted, using his fingers to whistle a sharp alert. "We need to get ourselves—"

The cheerful front door to the Jeffersons' burst open as Darnell stomped in, carrying something—no *someone*—under his arm, with Calamity hot on his heels. Someone who squirmed and fought like a tiger, but was incapable of escaping because of Darnell's tight grip on him.

He threw him in the middle of the living room floor at their feet like a bowling ball, as Darnell's victim screeched and whined whimpering protests. "Caught him just as that dude mowed down our girl and dang well disappeared. I ain't never seen nothin' like that. But Calamity froze this boy's sorry butt right on the spot, yo. Made for an easy catch."

The dude in question was Bradley. He skittered backward on his hands until he was pressed up against the brick of the enormous fireplace, his eyes wide with terror, his jeans torn. "Get away from me!" he screamed, his face red and bloodied.

"Where is my son!" Wanda screamed back, her eyes wild, her hair flying about her face, as she made a mad dash straight at him, but Greg, with catlike grace, caught her by the waist.

She struggled and twisted, but he held on to her. "Wanda!" he shouted at her, pulling her to him to calm her. "Stop! Please, just stop and let us help. What won't help is if you kill him."

Nina was at her husband's side in seconds, taking Wanda from him with surprisingly gentle hands. "Give her to me. Wanda, honey, I need you to think like the baby's a client, okay? Stop freaking out and help me help you."

Wanda stopped for a moment, hiccupping a breath before she buried her face in Nina's shoulder and, in what Grey guessed was an uncharacteristic trait, sobbed into her hoodie as Marty smoothed her hand over her back.

And while everyone was busy relocating Wanda to another room, Grey swooped in and grabbed Bradley by the shirt, hauling him upward until they were face to face then shaking him hard enough to make coins fall out of his pocket. He let his rage, his disbelief grip his sense of reason, and all he wanted to do was smash this fuck into a wall.

"If you don't tell me where that motherfucker is, I'll beat you until you're unrecognizable. Understand me, freak?"

Keegan was beside him in a flash of movement, placing a firm hand on his shoulder, giving him a touchstone to reality. "Grey, get a hold of yourself, man! You're making his damn teeth chatter. Put him down and let's get through this, then you can do whatever you want to this little weasel and I'll gladly look the other way."

Grey threw him back to the ground, his muscles clenching and flexing in release as he thought about not just the baby, but Sal.

Christ, he'd never be able to live with himself if someone hurt Sal.

Getting himself in check, he joined the men as they closed in on a terrified Bradley, their anger palpable.

"So, here's the way this is gonna go, pervert," Grey sneered at him while he sniveled and shrank away from their heated glances. "You tell me where they are, and I don't let everyone have a nice go at you and leave you for dead. Do we have a deal, *Bradley*?"

~

Sweet hell on fire. Sweet, sweet hell. She almost couldn't speak, and that wasn't just because her ribs ached so badly.

The face staring down at her, gorgeous and angular, was what took her breath away.

How? How could everyone have missed this? It was like hiding in plain sight.

"Oh, Sal. Have I shocked you? That's how everyone feels when they find out. You're not alone, pretty lady."

She wheezed air into her lungs and asked, "But *why?* Why this? Why Samantha?" All stupid questions to be sure. Questions she knew the answers to, but they popped out of her mouth anyway.

His face split into a grin, an evil, ugly grin. "Come on, Sal, surely you can't be that stupid. Samantha was a rare zombie. Do you have any idea how much men pay to spend ten minutes with a woman like that? If that's not get your freak on, then what is?"

"Did Bradley…did he force…"

"Did he force her into bed? Nah. She'd fallen for him hook, line and sinker by then. He had her believing they were going to run away together. Have a family, a picket fence and all the trimmings. She was so skittish at first, but once he reeled her in and she got pregnant, everything else was a breeze. Bradley was good, I'll give him that. One of my best groomers. Something about that shy, gawky things all the girls love. I'm gonna miss him. But he fucked up, Sal. So he had to go. I can't believe he let her get away, and then to top everything off, he fell for your bullshit baby swap. He might have been good at some things, but he had shit for brains."

"Samantha got away?" she squeaked.

He tipped his head back and laughed, flashing his brilliantly white teeth. "She sure did. Took the baby, too. Managed to get to a rest area, where she called you. Just before I killed her, that is. But damn Grey was quicker than I've ever given him credit for. Mr. Honorable got to the baby before I could get myself cleaned up. Samantha was a messy, messy death, you know. Ruined my favorite pair of shoes. Of course, you're boyfriend wanted to know how I knew where the baby was and I fed him some line about getting a tip from one of my deep cover informants. Then before I know it, the kid's in social services' hands and off to that damn orphanage. But it all worked out, didn't it?"

Horror hit her from head to toe at his words, but it wasn't just the words, or how callously he talked about Samantha dying, it was what was going to happen to *her*. She knew she was going to die, and she'd never see Grey or Buttercup or the baby again.

And that made her irate—infuriated he held so much control while he looked down at her, grinning like some twisted circus clown. But what could she do? As she looked around again, she realized she wasn't just in a hole, she was deep in the ground somewhere. So deep, she couldn't climb out if she tried. There was no way out unless someone threw her a rope.

So what does a girl do when she's going to die?

She puts all her shit on the table—all her anguish, all her hatred, everything.

Looking upward, she flipped him the bird and spat, "You sick fuck! What made you decide to sell women into slavery? What makes you take money from men who want to do sick things to a woman while she lies helpless, unable to stop the assault? Is it because you're a limp dick? Did mommy forget to cut the crust off your sandwiches, douchebag? Did that make you a sad boy? What makes a man force a woman to have sex with him unless he's a weak, spineless moron who can't get it up?"

Her words echoed around the hole she was in, swirling about her head, but his face changed from gleeful to angry for just a moment before he wagged a finger at her. "You don't think that's going to work on me like it did on that poor shit Bradley, do you, Sal? You're good, but you're not that good, honey. But you are damn nice to look at. So I guess you're about find out all about limp dicks, aren't you? You're going to bring me a pretty penny, Sally Brice. And so is he."

As quick as anything she'd ever seen, he produced the baby, who was miraculously sleping through it all, still swaddled in the blanket he'd been in that afternoon when she'd pressed a kiss to his soft forehead before going to meet Bradley.

Now her chest heaved, from terror, from rage, from the helplessness of it all. But the hell she was going down without a fight. She knew how this ended. She knew she was on her way out, but she wasn't going without the satisfaction of looking him in the eye and throwing him a curveball she hoped would freak him out enough to put him off balance. She hoped it would give Grey and the women of OOPS some time to figure this out—enough time to get them here to at least save the baby.

"Hey!" she shouted upward. "Remember that vision I had the other day?"

He tickled the baby under the chin and nodded with a smile. "Yep, I sure do. All that howling and carrying on is really quite something. Samantha did say it was loud, but that you're always accurate. She said that just a few days before I tore her to shreds."

Refusing to be goaded about how Samantha had died at his hands, she kept her voice steady and even. "Wanna know a something else?"

"I want to know everything, Sal. Absolutely everything about you, so I can put it on your resume on our website on the dark web," he said in a teasing tone.

Lifting her chin, her nostrils flaring, Sal asked, "Wanna know who died in that vision?"

He grinned as if this were some game. "I'm all pins and needles, edge of my seat, hottie."

"It was you, *Agent Carr*. It was you!"

CHAPTER 13

"Are you fucking kidding me, Bradley?" Nina gave him a hard shove between his thin shoulder blades before she jogged over the rough terrain in front of him. "We've been walking for miles. You'd goddamn well better be taking us to the right place, or I think you know what I'll do, don't you, human?" She flashed her fangs at a cringing, terrified Bradley.

"I swear this is the place!" he huffed, his words shaky. "This is exactly where he takes them before he ships them out to—"

"I think you mean where *you* take them, too, Bradley, don't you, Little Dick?" Nina goaded. "You sick, sick little boy. You helped the motherfucker, didn't you? I think…yes. I think that's exactly what you fucking told us. You sucked the girls in and got paid a nice percentage for it. Correct me if I'm wrong, but isn't that what Little Dick said, Darnell?"

Darnell grunted his disgust as he padded behind them. "You ain't wrong. That's what this pig said, Boss."

"Oh, Bradley, the shit I'm gonna do to you," Nina cooed, then cackled and winked.

His face crumpled. "Please, please let me go! I'll testify against him. I'll do whatever you ask me to do, but please let me go!" Bradley cried, stopping Grey in his tracks.

He grabbed the coward by the collar of his shirt and eyeballed him with venom. "That's not how it works in our world, Bradley. That's the human process of the judicial system. In our world, we kill you for what you've done, and we don't give a shit if you help us in the process. Either way, you're gonna die. If not by their hand, then by mine, and if I don't find Sal and the baby safe, if anything happens to them, it'll be slow, buddy. So slow and agonizingly painful while I peel your skin off layer by layer, you'll wish you'd ended it all yourself. I don't know how you got mixed up with all this—being a human—but your shit's about to hit a fan. Now walk!" he roared down at him.

"But—but—you promised!" he squealed in weak protest.

"He lied!" Wanda howled in his face. "Just like you lied to Samantha. Now walk or I'll eat your leg clear off your body!" She gave him a hard shove, jolting him forward.

She'd done exactly as Nina told her to do and had gotten it together in time to be helpful, and Grey had to admit, these people knew their shit when they worked as a team. Most especially the women.

He hadn't even contacted his superior McCall. There'd be too much red tape, too much explaining, too much of a chance Carr would live—and he didn't want him to live. He had the woman he loved. That meant he had to die and grey would suffer the repercussions later.

As the group moved forward out here in no man's land on hundreds of acres of woods a good distance from the city, adhering to the plan they'd made, Grey fought to keep his head on straight.

Carr. He couldn't believe it was Carr, but it explained so much. It explained how he'd always been one step ahead of them during this whole investigation, how Bradley had gotten away the night he'd attacked Sal.

Grey hadn't even questioned the idea that Carr was a werewolf and, up against a measly human, surely could have caught Bradley the night he hit Sal. He hadn't questioned it because he'd trusted his partner.

Though, now that he knew the full story, he had to admit he'd been surprised Carr hadn't killed Bradley himself for losing track of the baby. Though, Bradley had explained he'd hidden from Carr until the coast was clear, and then his plan was to try to snatch the baby and give him back to save his own nuts.

Yet, he'd saved Carr the trouble of actually having to kidnap the baby and produce him for whoever this buyer was just by lurking around the Jefferson's'. It gave them a reason to set up the sting and it gave Carr the opportunity to snatch the baby right out from under them

Then there was Sal. He wondered how Carr had felt when she came on the scene. Sal asking around about Samantha the way she did was only a small glitch in Carr's plans, according to Bradley.

Though, he hadn't counted on his partner becoming involved with Sal. That had thrown him off guard, and when Grey had come upon the texts and chat logs from Samantha and Bradley on his own, Carr had been thrown for another small loop.

Likely, he'd planned to get to Bradley first and kill him before Grey and their team could get their hands on him to interrogate. But then Bradley had gone into deep hiding, knowing Carr and his group would kill him because he'd lost the baby.

So the son of a bitch had played right along with the whole scheme to trick Bradley, leaving the baby wide open to snatching, and the opportunity for a perfect setting to kill Bradley in the process. Two birds, one stone.

And never once had Grey suspected. Never once.

The only thing they had going for them right now was Carr thought Bradley was dead. When Calamity had frozen him with a spell, one of Carr's brainless thugs had smelled him and mistook him for a goner.

"We're here," Bradley whispered into the dark night,

clear terror lacing his tone. "Over there. That's the shack he keeps them in. He has them in holes he dug in the floor until he moves them. There's no way out of there unless someone throws a rope down to them."

Jesus, Samantha must have felt completely helpless. The more Grey heard, the more he wanted to kill Carr.

Nina wrapped her arm around Bradley's neck and squeezed until his eyes bulged and his tongue fell out of his mouth. "Just like there's no way out for you, perv. Sucks to be helpless, huh?" Then she gave him a hard shove to the ground, where he crumpled into a pathetic ball.

Grey looked to the worn, half-falling-down cabin made of wood and pieces of plywood and clenched his jaw. It was swarming with goons armed with guns, pacing back and froth. Maybe twenty in total. But for sure they'd all have some element of strength.

Grey gathered them into a circle and went over the only hope they had at this point. The element of surprise.

"Okay, so you seven disarm that bunch of monkey's manning the outside of the shack. The only way in is to take them by surprise. Do whatever you have to do to get me inside. I'm no weakling, but I'm no werewolf or vampire either. You're all stronger by a long shot. But I have a big-ass gun and I'm not afraid to use it on Carr. Get me inside and I'll get Sal and the baby to safety. Are we all clear?"

Nina cracked her knuckles as everyone nodded

their understanding. "It's freak-huntin' time," she said with glee.

Greg dropped a kiss of approval on her forehead as he looked at her with admiration. "God, I love you, honey. Let's go kick some ass, Vampire."

"So this is how you spend your days with OOPS, babe?" Keegan asked.

Marty bit her bottom lip and glanced up at him sheepishly. "Not all of them. Just some. You were there when we saved Nina. You know what it's all about."

Keegan grinned at her, scooping her up to plant a kiss on her lips. "You do know you're pretty hot, don't you? Awesome and hot."

"Ditto," Heath echoed to Wanda.

"Calamity? You keep Bradley right here with whatever spell it takes, okay? Do not let him out of your sight—and keep his mouth shut," Grey ordered.

Stretching her paws to unsheathe her claws, Calamity circled a whimpering Bradley with dark menace. "Not a problem," she replied, walking up and over his hip to peer into his eyes. "Hey, Bradley, got a question for you. Cats or dogs?" Then she giggled like a giddy schoolgirl.

Grey looked to them all, concern for their safety at a premium. "Above all, be safe, folks. *Please* be safe. Ready? Set! Break!"

Nina grabbed him by the arm and pulled him aside as everyone began to assemble, her eyes solemn. "One thing before we go, Fifty Shades."

"What's that?"

"That vision your woman had—quick question? She did say that sometimes the people who are supposed to die in them can be saved, didn't she? Did I hear that shit right?"

He gave Nina a suspicious look. "Yeah. She told me that once, too."

"I got a bad feeling, Secret Agent Man. I just wanna be sure."

His skin began to crawl. "A bad feeling about what?"

"I'm just gonna say this straight up to you, due to the dire nature of this shit. She wouldn't tell us who it was, but I got a bad feeling she saw herself in that vision."

Jesus. Jesus Christ.

He clenched his jaw and gave a sharp nod. "Then let's make sure that doesn't happen."

Taking one last look at Samantha's picture, the one Sal had given him what felt like a million years ago, he ran on soft feet directly into the fray.

~

"Y*ou're lying!*" Carr spat, shifting to a sitting position at the edge of the crude hole as he rocked the baby with rough jerks.

"How would you know?" she taunted him, enjoying his brief look of surprise when he'd heard her speak those words.

His handsome face appeared to regain his former composure. "You'd say anything to get out of there."

"Would I? I didn't ask you to get me out of anywhere, did I, Agent Carr? Is this me begging for my life? Nope. No, it is not. Know why? Because my life's going to be just fine, you pig. It's yours that's in jeopardy. I saw it. I saw it all!" she bellowed, pushing her way up the wall to fully stand on legs like soft butter.

If a face could reflect true evil, uncontrollable rage, Carr cornered the market. "Shut up, you dumb bitch!"

"Make me!" she hollered back. "You're afraid aren't you, Agent Carr? Want me to tell you how you die? It's not pretty, sweetheart. Not pretty at all. But it's on its way. Aren't you even a little curious?" When he didn't bite, she egged him on some more. "C'mon, a big, strong, impotent guy like you can take it, can't you? Or are you just a big fat pussy?"

"Shut up or I'll throw this baby down there with you!" With those words, he held the baby up with both hands and let him hover over the hole.

Pushing aside her terror, setting aside her fear, she knew he wouldn't do that, just as she'd known Bradley would meet her after she'd boxed his ears that day in the bar. "Aw, the hell you will! That baby's big money, you fuck. It's your ass on the line if you hurt him. Not mine. Oh, but wait! Maybe that's how you end up dead, huh? You drop the baby and your sick fucking buyer murders you for killing his cash. Are you sure you still don't want to guess how you die?"

His face went ugly when he realized the risk he was taking, and as the baby began to wail, tearing her heart to pieces, he got really angry. "I swear to fuck, when I get your ass out of there, I'm going to hurt you like you've never been hurt before!"

"Carr?" a soft voice called from somewhere.

Sal's head swiveled upward, her eyes wide, her heart beating out of her chest.

"Carr? Where's Bradley?"

She blinked. *Samantha?*

That had been Samantha's voice she'd heard.

But it was the last thing she heard before all manner of hell broke loose.

Guns began firing, shots ringing out into the air, one after the other. Screams pierced her ears as chaos ensued. She couldn't see, but she heard as the structure began to crumble around her.

As she tried to look up amidst the debris falling on her, Carr was gone and so was the baby, making her pulse crash in her ears.

Whatever was happening up there, she prayed it was Grey and the women and men of OOPS, wreaking havoc on these pukes in order to save the baby.

Rocks began to shift and shake, crumbling around her in dusty pings of sound, pummeling her until all she could do was take cover under her arms.

Everything, all the sounds of the floor above creaking and shaking, the rocks and dirt falling from the walls, all of it was exactly like her vision.

But she didn't care about her demise; she only cared about the baby and his ultimate safety. Instead of fighting the inevitable, knowing there was no way out, she silently prayed for the baby, for Wanda and

Heath and all the people who'd fought so hard to protect him.

"Saaal!" someone screamed—someone who went by the nickname Marshmallow.

Her eyes lifted only briefly as she saw the vampire crash down beside her, landing on her feet, scooping Sal up, and hauling her over her shoulder.

"Cover your fucking eyes, kiddo!" she ordered on a yelp, bending at the knees and virtually leaping upward to the edge of the hole's ragged edges.

Dropping Sal on the floor of what appeared to be a ramshackle cabin, she yelled and pointed to a corner of the room where Carr held the baby, "I'll get the motherfucker, you get the baby, Sal! Get the baby and run! Get the fuck as far away from here as you can!"

Sal didn't know what gave her the strength to pull herself up off the floor while bullets whizzed by her head and burly men flew upward in the air as Heath, Keegan, Darnell and Greg tackled one man after the other.

Wanda and Marty had shifted, cornering two men, their teeth dripping saliva.

With her ribs on fire, her legs aching as though she'd run a marathon, she ducked behind whatever she could find to shield herself in order to make her way toward the baby and Carr.

The cabin wasn't very large, but it felt like the size of a football field as she fought her way across the floor, her eyes only on Carr. Searing heat consumed her limbs, pain tore at her muscles but she pushed and pushed until she was almost there.

And then she saw Samantha—and her heart almost stopped beating entirely.

"Give me the baby, Carr," she said, soft and low, her arms held stretched outward. "Give him to me."

Sal's mind tried to wrap around the fact that Samantha was standing right in front of her, close enough to reach out and touch, until she realized it wasn't Samantha at all.

It was Grey, and his own image was beginning to bleed through.

Which was when Carr realized it, too, but he realized it a half second too late, as Nina plowed into him, yelling the words, "Catch the baby!"

Oh shit, oh shit, oh shit!

The baby went flying in the air, up, up, up, as if in slow motion, tumbling, his terrified screams ringing in her ears. So she lunged with every ounce of energy she had left in her body, arcing upward in the air until she felt his soft form against her hands.

Sal cradled him to her, tucking him against her chest and clinging to him as he howled his discontent, just before she hit the ground with a thud.

Rolling to her side, she met Grey's eyes and that was when he bellowed, "Run, Sal! Run! Take the baby and run!"

Her ears heard the demand, but her feet didn't want to cooperate until she heard a snarl so vicious, so loud, she cringed in fear just before Carr, in werewolf form, launched himself at Grey and grabbed him by the throat.

Her stomach plummeted to her feet at the sight as Grey's blood spewed everywhere. Hot tears stung her eyes, and that was when she knew she had no choice but to move.

Tearing across the room, Darnell blocked one werewolf impeding her path by lifting him high in the air and slamming him to the ground with a howl. "Keep goin'! Go, Sal! Go!" he cried out as she stumbled over some fallen wood, ripped and hanging from the wall.

Her legs took over as she curled the baby into her and ran, only to hear that vicious snarl again, but this time it was right on her heels.

Oh, my God, she couldn't outrun a werewolf! She'd barely passed phys ed in high school. But his snuffing brought new life to her feet.

Sal saw the door leading to outside, saw Greg at the door, fighting to clear a path for her, and she charged, ran with everything she had in her. Close, she was so close as her lungs exploded and her chest heaved.

Just as she placed a foot out the door, she was knocked to the floor, sending her flying toward a wall. Curling into a ball, all she could do was huddle the baby close, turn her body sideways as she saw the wall coming straight for her face, and pray she was enough protection between him and the hard wood.

Sal crashed hard, hard and fast, making her whole body shudder, pushing her neck and spine to an awkward angle against the surface, and then Carr was on her, his face half human, half shifted into his were form.

He roared in her face, opening his mouth wide, the drool from his exceptionally long teeth hitting her skin in sticky beads. He was going to kill her, sink his teeth into her jugular and sever it, his heavy weight almost crushing her.

So she did the only thing she could think to do as she covered the baby's ears as tightly as possible without hurting him.

She opened her mouth, too, and screamed, screamed for all she was worth.

The sound pierced the glass window, shattering it into sharp splinters, spraying everyone in the vicinity.

It reverberated around the room, echoing, making all movement come to a halt. And then someone was yelling, maybe Darnell. "Stop, Sal! Stop! You're killing them!"

The moment she closed her mouth was the moment Wanda reanimated. Sal watched from the corner of her eye as her hind legs pumped and her jaws opened wide.

She rammed into Carr with the force of a tornado, knocking him to his back and going for his throat. But he was a mere second quicker than her as he howled out in rage, hurling Wanda off him, rolling to his side and rising to stand on only two feet.

And as he came at Sal again, stalking across the floor in a freakish display of tufts of hair and legs with paws, he screamed, "I'll kill you, you bitch!"

Terror coursed through her veins, fear threatened

to hold her down like an anchor as she tried to scramble back to her feet, all while the baby screamed.

"Get the fuck away from her, Carr, or I'll kill you!!"

Grey? Grey was alive? Oh, thank God, Grey was alive!

He threw himself between Sal and Carr, his stance wide, and then he pulled out something shiny and pointed it at Carr. "Stop, Carr, or I swear to fuck, I'll shoot!"

Carr bent his head, huffed one last huff, and then he charged at them like some raging, demented bull—just a half second before Grey pulled the trigger, hitting him square in the head.

The werewolf fell to the ground in a heap of half-morphed limbs and hair, rocking the entire floor of the shack when he crashed.

And then he was still.

~

Grey knelt beside her, brushing the hair from her face with gentle hands. "Jesus Christ, Sal. Are you injured? Shot?"

She held the baby tight to her chest as he screamed, sure he hated being smothered, but she clung to him anyway as she squeezed her eyes shut and her heart finally began to slow.

"I think every bone in my body is broken, and I'm pretty sure I'm not winning any marathons after that sad attempt to outrun a werewolf. I need to hit a gym pronto."

Grey barked a laugh and pulled her and the baby close, pressing a tender kiss to her forehead. "I can't ever remember being so damn scared, Sal. You were amazing."

She gave him a weak laugh as she tried to sit up. "Tell that to him. He doesn't seem too pleased with me right now."

"Oh, Sal!" Wanda cried out, dropping to her knees as Nina draped her hoodie over her friend. She pressed her forehead to Sal's. "You saved him. You're a bloody miracle. Thank you, thank you, thank you," she whispered hoarsely.

Nina smiled down at her and gave her a thumb's up. "You're badass, Screamer, but fuck all, that thing you do is killer on the ears, dude."

Sal laughed as she let Wanda take the baby from her and Marty helped her sit, pulling her into a hug that made Sal wince a little, but she welcomed it anyway. "I'll never forget what you did for my friend, Sal. Not ever. I don't care what anyone says, you're as tough as we are."

Sal frowned playfully, ignoring the screaming pain in her ribs as Grey helped her to stand. "Who said I'm not as tough as you guys? Was it the big ol' marshmallow here?"

Nina made a big stink of growling fiercely at her, but she gave her hand a tight squeeze and mouthed the words *thank you* before stepping back to lean against Greg.

Darnell enveloped her in a warm bear hug and chuckled. "Aw, Sal. I love that you're willin' to poke the bear. Shows grit, girl. Real grit."

Heath put a hand on her shoulder and looked down at her, his eyes serious. "I don't have the words to express my gratitude for what you've done, Sal, but no matter when, no matter where, if you ever need me, all you have to do is say the word."

Sal's cheeks went hot, but she managed an embarrassed smile of acknowledgement before giving him a quick hug.

"All right, we've embarrassed Sal enough," Keegan said as he gripped her shoulder in a brief gesture. "I call we take Sal and this little guy and his mother home. I'd bet Arch has some leftover cake, and I don't know about you, but I worked up an appetite." He rubbed his flat belly, making everyone laugh.

"And while we're at it, we need to give this poor baby a name, Wanda Schwartz-Jefferson!" Nina yelled

As everyone drifted out of the shack, talking and laughing, and Grey's team, who as instructed, Calamity had called, rounded up whoever was still left standing, Sal held back for a minute, taking one last look at the place she knew in her heart Samantha had been kept. In a filthy hole, waiting to be sold to the highest freak bidder.

Grey wrapped her in his arms and rested his chin on the top of her head. "Don't, Sal."

She shook her head against his chest, squeezing her eyes shut to thwart her tears. "I don't know if I can bear it, Grey."

Tipping her chin upward, he wiped the tears that managed to slide down her cheeks anyway, with his thumbs. "I'll help you, honey. I'll help, okay?"

"Okay," she whispered, standing on tiptoe to press a soft kiss to his lips before she moaned in pain.

"Sounds like somebody needs a good rubdown with some Icy Hot."

"I need to be dipped in a vat of it. Just roll me around in it. I'm pretty sure I'm never going to walk right again, and that reminds me, would you check my spine? I think my liver is now housed there."

He laughed at her, his eyes warm as he took her hand. "Dr. Grey, at your service. C'mon, let's go see a man about how much a vat of Icy Hot'll run me."

She giggled and gingerly followed behind him with slow, stilted steps. "Oooo, are you buying, skinwalker? If that's the case, make that a double."

"What better way to celebrate new beginnings than with some Icy Hot?" he asked, stopping to kiss the tip of her nose.

"Is this a new beginning?" she asked, suddenly shy.

"Yep. So let's start at the beginning. I'm Grey Hamlin, skinwalker, paranormal agent, and big vat-buying spender. Nice to meet you."

She grinned, her heart lighter than it had been for quite some time, despite her all-over body ache. "The pleasure is all mine. I'm Sal Brice, lame bartender in a dive bar, photographer and sketch artist-slash-hobbyist, and a banshee, better known as a really loud screamer."

Grey's laugh was hearty as they stepped out of the shack.

Directly into their brand-new beginning.

EPILOGUE

Two months later on a lovely day in July...

One banshee, aka, The Screamer who'd found a family to call her own; an incredibly hot, semi-retired paranormal FBI agent/skinwalker, happy to lay down some roots for the first time in his adult life; a half vampire, half witch who secretly loves being called Marshmallow; a pretty blonde werewolf who isn't entirely quite sure how to teach a boy baby how to outlet mall shop, but continues to devise a plan to bring said dream to fruition; a halfsie, overjoyed new mother with yet another secret to share; a sort of greenish baby who's slowly, to his parents' great relief, in the process of being weaned off brains; a manservant who makes the creamiest bacon mac and cheese ever and plans to show everyone what's what when he dresses up as a pimp at Halloween; a demon who has big plans to teach a baby zombie the joys of football and chicken wings; a snarky cat who's becoming more OOPS-centric everyday; a gentle zombie who has a new best buddy zombie baby; happy, healthy children in every nook and cranny of a big farmhouse; baseball-watching spouses; and more accidental clients and their families than anyone can keep track of anymore, gathered together to celebrate a very special someone who, while not present, will always be worthy of a celebration…

"Look at you!" Wanda crowed at her as she grabbed Sal's hand at her front door and spun her around, puffing the skirt of her sundress outward. "You look amazing—so glowing and happy! I'm so glad you two are here!"

"You know what that means, don't ya, Wanda? It means she's doing the humpty-hump on the reg with ex-Agent Fifty Shades," Nina teased, yanking Sal into a hug. "How are ya, kiddo?"

Sal smiled up at Nina and gave her a hug right back. She'd grown used to them doting on her over the last two months. One of them was always showing up at her shitty apartment door, pushing their way in to bring her food and DVDs and medicine as she healed from her run-in with Carr at the shack.

As it so happened, she'd ended up with three

broken ribs, a fractured skull, two sprained fingers and a twisted ankle. Needless to say, the vat of Icy Hot was taken off the table in favor of X-rays and Ace bandages.

"I'm feeling really good, Marshmallow. How's you?"

"You mean since the last time you made me sit through that fucking marathon of *iZombie* just a week ago? Which is all a load bullshit, by the way. Hollywood's so fucked up."

Sal smoothed Nina's hoodie over her shoulder and smiled. "I think you said that, and you also said it beat shopping with these two pains in the ass and you'd watch ten marathons with me if it meant you didn't have to suffer through another scarf-buying spree."

"Touché, Screamer," the vampire said with a cackle.

"Sal!" Marty flew in from the dining room in a pretty sapphire-blue maxi dress and her signature bangle bracelets. She gave Sal a tight squeeze before setting her from her and gazing intently into her eyes. "Did you try that facial I brought you, young lady? You're simply glowing!"

Sal finally understood Arch's crack about Bobbie Sue and Pack Cosmetics, because she was now the proud owner of every face cream, lotion, perfume, eyeshadow and so on from each company, all presented to her in a gift basket so big, Buttercup almost had to get her own apartment.

Nina made a face at her friend. "That's not why she's glowing, Marty. She's doin' her dude. Leave her be already."

Marty batted at Nina's hands. "Hush, vampire. Don't embarrass our girl."

Grey cleared his throat and stuck a hand in the air. "You do know I'm here, too, right? You know, the guy allegedly responsible for the glow?"

The women's laughter peeled throughout the room and they all slapped him on the back. "How are you, Grey? Feeling more relaxed now that you've semi-retired?" Wanda asked.

He dropped a kiss on her cheek and smiled. "I'm feeling really, really good, Wanda. Better than I have in years, in fact. You look great, by the way. Motherhood agrees with you."

True to his words, he was feeling good. Grey had decided to leave undercover work and take the role of part-time consultant for now, something he could pick and choose if a case came up. They'd spent many nights not just getting to know one another, but talking about what happened the night in the cabin.

Carr's betrayal had cut Grey deeply, and upon closer introspection after a case so ugly, he'd decided now was the time to make a move to something gentler. He'd seen a lot as an agent, a lot of brutality, a lot of heartache, but the trafficking had taken the wind right out of his sails.

"So, how's the painting going, young lady?" Marty asked, her eyes bright.

After seeing a batch of her sketches and pictures, the women of OOPS, along with Grey, had encouraged her to pursue her passion.

"Did she tell you?" Grey asked, his tone laced with pride as he squeezed her hand. "She got her first showing at some artsy-fartsy place in the village. Can't tell you how proud I am of her. She's going to be a superstar in the art world."

She had indeed gotten a showing. In fact, she had two at yet another artsy-fartsy place in the village, and she couldn't have been more thrilled.

With Grey and the girls' support, she'd taken the bull by the horns and showed some of her pictures and paintings to some art dealers, and lo and behold, Sal Brice was no longer a shitty bartender. She was an artist. Still a little starving, but an artist just the same.

The three women squealed their approval—well, except Nina. She didn't squeal in excitement about anything unless it involved killing people. But she did give Sal a good slap on the back.

Speaking of killing people, Bradley was in prison—paranormal prison—where he hoped to appeal his quick conviction, and the agency Grey worked for continued to keep him alive to glean more information out of him until they had every last one of the people involved in the trafficking organization.

And she could live with that. She'd wanted him dead, but if he was more useful alive, she'd find a way to deal.

As for her and Grey, their relationship had deepened, intensified, grew more intimate in more ways than just the physical. Each day brought new revelations about each other, each day they helped one another heal, each day he helped her to accept her visions, which were fewer and further between lately. Each day Sal felt more and more like this was forever for her, and she couldn't have been happier.

To be honest, she'd fallen head over heels, and Grey had told her the same thing just last night as they ate Twinkies and drank wine on the balcony of the new apartment they'd just moved into two days ago —together.

There were still days she ached that Samantha wasn't here to share her joy—to see how her dream had come true in the way they'd always talked about. But it was getting easier to accept this newfound happiness and the people who'd shown her it was okay to love someone back.

Wrapping her arm around Wanda, Sal asked, "So, where's that baby? Auntie Sal needs a smooch. Lead the way, lady!"

Wanda had brought the baby over all the time to visit her as she'd recuperated, honoring the bond between them, and he was thriving and growing and as perfect as any baby could be.

Entering the dining room, where heaps of food on platters sat on the long table, she was greeted by Heath, Keegan, Greg, Carl and Darnell, all smiling as they each gave her a quick kiss and hug.

Sometimes, Sal had to pinch herself when she saw so many people genuinely happy to see her. It filled her heart with so much joy, she was sure the organ would burst from her chest.

The baby sat in a bouncy seat, his fingers clutched around a blue rattle, a pacifier clipped to his adorable overalls. Sal dropped a loving kiss on his forehead, noting how much more he looked like Samantha every time she saw him.

Wanda grabbed a champagne glass and clinked it with a fork, a warm smile on her face. "Ladies and gentleman—I'd like to propose a toast, and make a couple of announcements. First, thank you for being here. You know how much we love all of you and how important it is for you to share this special day. Next, raise your glasses to Sal. A lady who's become so very special to me and my family—to all of us, actually." Wanda tilted her glass in Sal's direction, making her tuck herself against Grey's side out of embarrassment.

"To Sal!" Heath called out.

But Wanda wasn't done, her blue eyes shiny with unshed tears. "And also to Samantha Carter, the single most courageous woman I've ever known. I honor her every day in my heart and thank her over and over for the blessing she gave Heath and I. So we hope you'll join us in officially welcoming little Samuel Carter Schwartz-Jefferson!"

A cheer went up from the crowded dining room, packed with people, and Nina yelled out, "It's about time you gave the kid a name!" making everyone laugh.

Tears sprang to the corner of Sal's eyes when, to add to her delight, Heath unveiled a gorgeous silver picture frame, showcasing a picture of Samantha that Sal had taken, her smile warm, her beautiful eyes glowing with all the hope and joy she'd spread to anyone who knew her. He ceremoniously hung it on the wall, right next to the rest of the Jefferson family photos.

Wanda truly was the nicest person she'd ever met, and Sal said as much when she crossed the room and threw herself at her, hugging her hard. "I wish she were here to see this—to feel it. She would have loved you all so much."

Wanda tugged at Sal's braid with a smile. "Oh, I think she's here, honey. I think she'll always be here in one manner or another. I'll make sure of it."

Grey came up behind her and placed his hands on her shoulders. "Any more announcements or are we getting some of Arch's cake?" he teased.

"Just one more," Heath said with a secretive smile as he looked to Wanda, and she nodded her head. "I'd ask you all to raise your glass one more time. To Wanda, my beautiful wife and the mother to not just one of my children, but two!"

There was a moment of silence as everyone digested what Heath said, and then Wanda cried, "I'm pregnant!"

And everyone erupted in cheers of pleasure and congratulations again as Grey enveloped Sal in a warm embrace and people laughed and hugged each other.

More than ever before, Sal knew she'd found her forever—with Grey, with the women and men of OOPS.

Right here in suburbia.

The End

I so hope you've enjoyed Wanda's journey into motherhood, and I also hope you'll rejoin me and the ladies of OOPS for yet another adventure, The Accidental Mermaid! Coming really, really soon!

PREVIEW ANOTHER BOOK BY DAKOTA CASSIDY

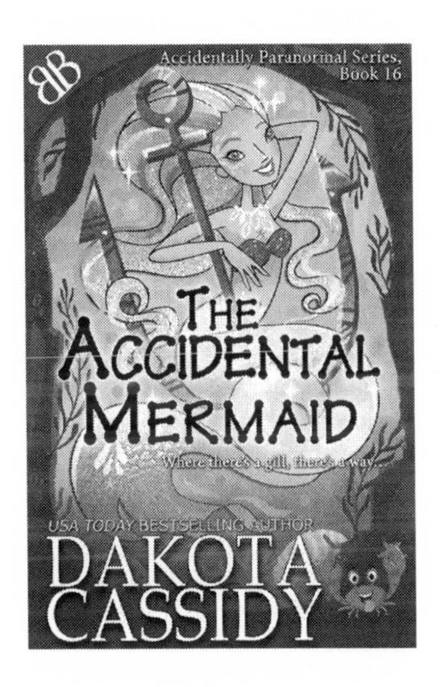

Chapter 1

"On the real?" the dark-haired, eerily pale woman—wearing a hoodie and a T-shirt that read "Not Today,

Satan" with slim-fitting jeans—asked her very pregnant friend. Who, by the way, dressed like Grace Kelly and smelled like a luscious rose garden.

"Yes, Nina. On the real."

"Like a tail, and scales, and one of those little beaded B-cup bras?"

The pregnant woman sucked in her cheeks, her nostrils flaring. "No beaded bra, but definitely a tail. It's quite beautiful, in fact. I mean, as tails and scales go."

"So lemme see, Wanda," she insisted with a pleading tone that held a hint of strangely malicious glee. Her beautiful eyes gazed curiously as she peeked over her friend's shoulder from the hallway leading off the changing rooms.

But Wanda put five pale-polished nails to the woman's shoulder and shook her head. "Only if you promise not to stare and make rude jokes."

"Don't be a moron. Of course I'm gonna stare and make rude jokes, Wanda. She has a fucking tail, dude. She's in the middle of a public pool floor, under the stairs to the diving board, no frickin' less. Who *wouldn't* stare at that shit?"

"*Nina…*" the woman said with a warning tone, her high cheekbones turning a pretty pink.

Wanda and Nina—both very nice, solid names. It's always pleasant to have a name to attach to the people talking about you and your "predicament" as though you're not even in the same room…while you're on the floor…literally flopping around, looking for cover.

Nina, holding an equally beautiful dark-haired little

girl with curly hair and the cherubic face of an angel, wearing the sweetest purple tutu swimsuit with ballerinas on the chest, pushed her way past the pregnant Wanda at the entry to the pool. She looked down to the blue-tiled surface of the flooring where Esther Williams Sanchez lay.

And then her mouth fell open.

Immediately afterward, she clamped her mouth shut and her shoulders slumped in a pouty way. "Is this another wormhole, Wanda? Like Shamalot? I don't wanna go back today. I have shit to do, and it always takes days for me to readjust to the time zones. It's like fairytale jetlag, dude."

A woman with long, glistening blonde hair, styled similarly to a Kardashian's, skidded into the pool area on a pair of burnt-orange heels so high, Esther thought surely she'd pitch headfirst into the pool. And then she thought what a shame that would be, because all that beautiful fake blonde hair would undoubtedly turn green if the pool's chemicals were to touch it.

"Ho-lee fucksticks!" the blonde shouted, her words echoing in the chlorine-scented air as she stopped just short of the tall dark-haired Goddess, who grabbed her by the arm to steady her and keep her from falling into the pool. "Is she a...?"

Nina, obviously recuperated, said, "No, Marty. She's not. This is all just a big fucking joke because that's how we roll at Mommy and Me swim class. We prank each other all the time. Last week, we fucked with all the moms by telling them we found Nemo in the pool."

Marty rolled her sapphire-blue eyes and let out a ragged sigh, cupping the back of her neck and massaging it with her fingers. "Shut it with the sarcasm, Dark Overlord, and tell me what happened. I have a headache the size of your mouth and I'm tired. It was a long day at Bobbie-Sue." Leaning over, she dropped a kiss on the baby's forehead and smiled. "Did you find something awesome at swim class, Charlie Girl? Who's Auntie Marty's favorite genie princess?" she asked the baby.

The baby answered with a squeal of joy, holding her arms out for her aunt to take her from her mother. Which Marty did, pressing kisses to the baby's chubby fists, making her coo with delight. Then she looked at the women named Wanda. "Her tail is spectacular, don't you think? And that hair! I'd kill a bitch to be in this kind of humidity and still have it fall all down my shoulders in those luscious rainbow curls."

Wanda eyed her tail and fins, the iridescent scales shimmering in a pale yellow and melting into shades of aqua and teal, and nodded. "It truly is magic."

"It's fucking yellow," Nina muttered.

Marty smiled distractedly at Nina before her face became serious. "So, what do we have so far, girls? How the heck did this happen?"

Esther squirmed uncomfortably. Well, she tried to squirm uncomfortably, but her tail (her tail!) made it almost impossible to move due to its heft and length. Also, if she moved the wrong way, her suddenly luxurious rainbow-colored hair would reveal her very naked breasts.

Wanda, with the swollen belly, dressed in a light blue maternity dress and conservative yet fashionable low heels, shook her head. "We don't know. I tried to talk to her, but she clammed up." Then she looked to Esther with her soft brown eyes, made up quite tastefully in pastel eyeshadow colors. "No pun intended, of course."

Clam up. Hah! Well, if nothing else, they had a sense of humor. Esther had a sense of humor, too. Which is one of the reasons why she'd agreed to take the Mommy and Me class for first-time swimmers—the only class they had available at the Y at this time of year, now that summer was over and fall classes had begun.

She'd taken it at the urging of her friend Juanita, because Esther was thirty-two years old, couldn't swim, and she was tired of hearing her friends tease her when they went to Mexico for impromptu vacations and she sat on the beach all alone due to her fear.

Marty eyed Esther with a critical glance. "Any idea why a woman of her age is taking a class at Mommy and Me?" She paused and then gasped. "Wait! Is there a child involved here? Where's the child? Oh, hell. Please tell me there's not a baby in the mix, Wanda."

Wanda shook her head and picked invisible lint from Marty's sharp beige suit before straightening her dark brown and rust scarf. "No children involved in the making of this…this…whatever this is. I mean, I know what this is, but you know what I mean. I did manage to get that much out of her before she stopped talking to me. So, I'm not sure why she's at a Mommy and Me class."

Marty sighed, now massaging her forehead as she looked to Nina. "Did Big Mouth scare her? How many times have I told you when you find yourself in a position where someone is afraid, don't make them *more* afraid, Nina?"

The beautiful Nina pushed her hoodie from her head and flicked Marty's arm, taking the baby back. "Shut your Botoxed lips, Blondie. I haven't said jack shit. I was handing off Sam to Heath when all this went down. Speaking of, we better send him home with the kids so we can spend the next nine frillion hours of my life listening to the fish cry and carry on about how awful this is."

Wanda looked up from her phone. "I just texted him. He was in the parking lot waiting for me. And please, Nina, don't be so crude. You'll make her think we don't care. Plus, it's not like you don't have nine-frillion hours. You, my dear, have eternity."

Sam must be the baby with the strange complexion Nina had been carrying around in the pool along with her little girl Charlie. He was quite small, in Esther's opinion, for a swim class. But then, who was she to talk? She was in her thirties and still afraid of bathtub water deeper than four inches.

A tall, devastatingly handsome man with dark hair and gorgeous eyes, wearing a casual navy-blue pullover shirt and low-slung jeans, appeared behind Nina, carrying Sam. He put a hand to Wanda's waist and asked in a husky tone, "Trouble, honey?"

She patted his cheek lovingly and smiled, pressing a kiss to the baby's cheek and nuzzling his button nose. "Or something."

"Remember what we discussed, okay? Please?" he reminded her in a tone that spoke of a serious conversation they'd had.

Wanda smiled coquettishly at Heath and batted her eyelashes, rubbing her belly. "Promise, no heavy lifting today. I have to watch out for junior. He's my first priority. Always."

"First, that's my *daughter* you're carrying around. And that's not what you said when you picked up the car to collect Sam's teething ring, young lady," he teased good-naturedly.

Picked up the car? Like, the car-car or a toy car?

"Oh, stop. The SUV's not that heavy. I certainly wasn't crawling under it with this belly, and that's Sam's favorite teething ring. How could I leave it there until you got back from your golf game? And this?" She pointed to her belly. "Is a boy, Heath Jefferson."

Okay, So Wanda had picked up a car-car. Not a toy car.

What the fresh hell?

Standing on tiptoe, Wanda kissed her husband's lips. "You take the children home, would you, please? I promise to be very careful. No heavy lifting. Okay?"

Nina nudged Heath's wide shoulder. "Don't worry. I

got her back. We won't let her do anything she shouldn't do. Text Greg before you leave and he'll come get Charlie from you. Carl'll worry if she's gone for too long, and Calamity'll have a cow if Carl gets upset." Nina plopped kisses on each baby's forehead and waved them off.

"Stop being a worrywart, Heath. Would we, in a million years, let anything happen to Wanda and baby Jefferson? Never. We got this," Marty said, blowing kisses to the babies and waving to Heath before she turned around and narrowed her gaze on Esther, like she had a purpose and Esther was her mission.

Esther, who still hadn't spoken a word, fought a cringe under Marty's scrutiny.

As a general rule, she liked to observe people, situations, life, more than she liked to interact. At least at first. Her job as a divorce mediator required she pay close attention to body language and inflection and all sorts of things. But right now, after what had happened when she'd been the last in the class to climb out of the pool, she didn't have any words left to offer.

Instead, she'd just sit here under the diving board until this *thing* attached to her like some sort of colorful, yet, admittedly beautiful growth went away. It *would* go away, right? It had to go away...

On a sigh, Wanda slipped her arm through Marty's and they made their way the short distance to the diving board.

Marty sat on her haunches and looked at Esther

with the prettiest sapphire-blue eyes Esther had ever seen. "I'm Marty Flaherty. What's your name?"

"Swear to fuck, if it's Ariel, I'll piss myself," Nina cackled, coming to stand behind her friends.

Marty reached behind her back and swatted Nina's leg without even looking. "Find your inner marshmallow, Elvira, and show some empathy," she ordered, as though the order made any sense at all.

Now Wanda gazed at her, genuine concern on her finely boned face. "You're frightening us, honey. Please say something. We want to help. I promise you, we can help if you'll let us."

Yet, Esther cringed, attempting to inch farther away. After everything she'd heard, she was convinced these people were either all part of some weird cult of unbelievably pretty people who believed they had superpowers, like super-strength, or she was having a nightmare. A stone-cold, really real, scary-AF nightmare.

"Fuck, Wanda. Am I gonna have to haul this chick out to the car?" Nina complained, as though she hauled chicks with multicolored tails every day. "Because I'm tellin' ya, Marty's gonna have to move that shit-show of Bobbie-Sue crap out of the backseat. Her car's the biggest one we have, and we'll never stuff her ass in there with all that lip gloss."

Suddenly, and quite without warning, Esther found her voice. "Bobbie-Sue? Do you sell Bobbie-Sue?" She'd sold Bobbie-Sue once, in order to pay for college.

She'd been about as bad at it as a breast implant

salesman at a porn convention, worse at trying to put all that makeup on her face, let alone anyone else's. All that talk of color wheels and blend, blend, blend was not her gift.

Marty smiled warmly, her eyes lighting up. "She speaks! Yay! Now we're getting somewhere. And I *own* Bobbie-Sue, honey. I'm an honest, reputable businesswoman. And my husband owns Pack Cosmetics. We're in the process of merging the two companies right now. Which is why I missed Mommy and Me class tonight with my little girl, Hollis. But now you can see, you have nothing to be afraid of."

Tentatively gazing at the women, Esther confessed, "I tried to sell Bobbie-Sue to help pay for some college courses."

"Yeah, and you bought what with that pile of cash, a pack of pencils? Some Ramen noodles for a week?" Nina asked on a cynical snort.

"Actually, it was a loaf of bread and a bottle of mustard from the Andes. Did you know they even had their own mustard in the Andes?"

Marty shook her head and clucked her tongue. "Sounds like you didn't work the program... What's your name?"

"I'm not sure I want to tell you because I'm pretty sure you'll laugh." After that Ariel crack, she *knew* they would.

"Aw, they won't laugh," Nina reassured her. "I will, for damn sure. Trust and believe. But these two sensitive snowflakes would rather die than hurt your fucking feelings."

Giving them all a sheepish glance, she winced even before she spoke. "It's Esther…"

Wanda leaned in, her eyes questioning. "Esther…?" she coaxed with a hopeful glance.

She swallowed, smoothing her hands over the long length of her new locks. *Just say it and get it over with. You've lived with it all your life, for pity's sake.*

Well, sure I have. But that was just a bunch of lame jokes about being named after a famous synchronized swimmer and not actually being able to swim.

It wasn't because I had a tail with a fin.

"Esther Williams…er, Sanchez. Esther Williams Sanchez," she finally blurted out.

There was a short silence while each woman processed who Esther Williams was as the lights from the pool played against the ceiling and the floor continued to dry around her.

"Like the famous synchronized swimmer?" Nina crowed, holding her belly before she doubled over at the waist.

And then they all began to laugh.

Wanda was the first to recover, sputtering against the back of her hand and using her thumb to wipe tears from her eyes. "Ladies! Stahhp!" And then she choked out another string of hyena-ish giggles before she straightened and cleared her throat, composing herself. "Girls. Knock it off! There's someone in need. Also," she said, her eyes imploring Esther's, "please forgive me for behaving so poorly. I'm given to fits and spurts of all sorts of crazy emotions since I got knocked up. I wasn't laughing *at* you."

"But I wasn't laughing," Esther protested, catching a glimmer of her yellow and aqua tail under the pool lights before briefly clenching her eyes shut.

Wanda bit her lip to keep from laughing again. "Okay. I was laughing *at* you. But you have to admit, it's kind of funny, your name being…and you ending up a mermaid." Wanda shook her head as if it would help clear it. "Never mind. My apologies for being so rude."

Esther watched this all play out, but simply said, "No sweat."

Marty plopped down on the ground, holding her belly after laughing too hard, then she reached out a hand and placed it on Esther's arm. "I'm sorry, too. Now let's get down to business, Esther Williams Sanchez. How did this happen?"

"I'm *not* sorry, 'cuz that shit's funny, but yeah. How the fuck did this happen? Like, how do you have legs one minute and a tail the next?" Nina inquired.

Esther stared at the length of her body, and then she looked up at the ladies, all expectantly waiting for her to answer. The pressure to explain became intense. "I…I don't…"

Tears began to form in the corner of her eyes and panic swelled in her chest. Her heart raced, crashing against her ribs until she thought surely it would burst through the wall of her chest.

Nina rasped a sigh, planting her hands on her hips. "Fuck. Here we go, girlies. Meltdown in three, two—"

And then Esther screamed.

She screamed loud. So loud, it reverberated around the Olympic-size swimming pool, swirling and swishing as it wended its way into one ear and out the other.

And she didn't even care if she came off as some hysterical, screeching shrew—something she despised in most women.

She had a tail.

A fin.

A whateverthehell you wanted to label it.

She had it and it was attached to her and she didn't know how to get away from it.

So, she gulped in a fresh breath of air and screamed again.

Even louder.

NOTE FROM DAKOTA

I do hope you enjoyed this book, I'd so appreciate it if you'd help others enjoy it, too.

Recommend it. Please help other readers find this book by recommending it.

Review it. Please tell other readers why you liked this book by reviewing it at online retailers or your blog. Reader reviews help my books continue to be valued by distributors/resellers. I adore each and every reader who takes the time to write one!

If you love the book or leave a review, please email **dakota@dakotacassidy.com** so I can thank you with a personal email. Your support means more than you'll ever know! Thank you!

ABOUT THE AUTHOR

Dakota Cassidy is a USA Today bestselling author with over thirty books. She writes laugh-out-loud cozy mysteries, romantic comedy, grab-some-ice erotic romance, hot and sexy alpha males, paranormal shifters, contemporary kick-ass women, and more.

Dakota was invited by Bravo TV to be the Bravo-holic for a week, wherein she snarked the hell out of all the Bravo shows. She received a starred review from Publishers Weekly for Talk Dirty to Me, won a Romantic Times Reviewers' Choice Award for Kiss and Hell, along with many review site recommended reads and reviewer top pick awards.

Dakota lives in the gorgeous state of Oregon with her real-life hero and her dogs, and she loves hearing from readers!

OTHER BOOKS BY DAKOTA CASSIDY

Visit Dakota's website at
http://www.dakotacassidy.com for more information.

A Lemon Layne Mystery, a Contemporary Cozy Mystery Series

1. Prawn of the Dead
2. Play That Funky Music White Koi
3. Total Eclipse of the Carp

Witchless In Seattle Mysteries, a Paranormal Cozy Mystery series

1. Witch Slapped
2. Quit Your Witchin'
3. Dewitched
4. The Old Witcheroo
5. How the Witch Stole Christmas
6. Ain't Love a Witch
7. Good Witch Hunting

Nun of Your Business Mysteries, a Paranormal Cozy Mystery series

1. Then There Were Nun
2. Hit and Nun

Wolf Mates, a Paranormal Romantic Comedy series

1. An American Werewolf In Hoboken
2. What's New, Pussycat?
3. Gotta Have Faith
4. Moves Like Jagger
5. Bad Case of Loving You

A Paris, Texas Romance, a Paranormal Romantic Comedy series

1. Witched At Birth
2. What Not to Were
3. Witch Is the New Black
4. White Witchmas

Non-Series

Whose Bride Is She Anyway?

Polanski Brothers: Home of Eternal Rest

Sexy Lips 66

Accidentally Paranormal, a Paranormal Romantic Comedy series

Interview With an Accidental—a free introductory guide to the girls of the Accidentals!

1. The Accidental Werewolf
2. Accidentally Dead
3. The Accidental Human
4. Accidentally Demonic
5. Accidentally Catty
6. Accidentally Dead, Again

7. The Accidental Genie
8. The Accidental Werewolf 2: Something About Harry
9. The Accidental Dragon
10. Accidentally Aphrodite
11. Accidentally Ever After
12. Bearly Accidental
13. How Nina Got Her Fang Back
14. The Accidental Familiar
15. Then Came Wanda
16. The Accidental Mermaid

The Hell, a Paranormal Romantic Comedy series

1. Kiss and Hell
2. My Way to Hell

The Plum Orchard, a Contemporary Romantic Comedy series

1. Talk This Way
2. Talk Dirty to Me
3. Something to Talk About
4. Talking After Midnight

The Ex-Trophy Wives, a Contemporary Romantic Comedy series

1. You Dropped a Blonde On Me
2. Burning Down the Spouse
3. Waltz This Way

Fangs of Anarchy, a Paranormal Urban Fantasy series

1. Forbidden Alpha
2. Outlaw Alpha

Made in the USA
Middletown, DE
20 November 2018